THE ULTIMATE
SAN FRANCISCO 49ERS
TRIVIA BOOK

A Collection of Amazing Trivia Quizzes
and Fun Facts for Die-Hard 49ers Fans!

Ray Walker

<u>Exclusive Free Book</u>

Crazy Sports Stories

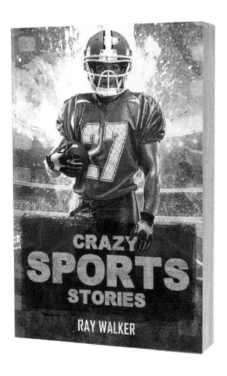

As a thank you for getting a copy of this book I would like to offer you a free copy of my book Crazy Sports Stories which comes packed with interesting stories from your favorite sports such as Football, Hockey, Baseball, Basketball and more.

Grab your free copy over at
<u>RayWalkerMedia.com/Bonus</u>

CONTENTS

INTRODUCTION

The San Francisco 49ers were the NFL's most dominant team in the 1980s, energizing a strong fan base around the Bay Area. People enjoy cheering for winners, and there was a lot of roars for the 49ers from 1981 through 1995 as San Francisco became the first team to win five Super Bowls. There have been plenty of chances to cheer on the 49ers in recent years as well, especially this past season, in 2019, when the 49ers advanced all the way to the Super Bowl behind the strong play of Jimmy Garoppolo.

The names of famous 49ers are among the best in the sport's history from quarterbacks Joe Montana and Steve Young to wide receiver Jerry Rice and safety Ronnie Lott. You'll learn more about all of them, how they arrived in San Francisco, and all the plethora of records they hold. You'll also learn about the team's origins, its most promising young players, and some of those names you almost forgot played for the 49ers.

This book is designed to test the most die-hard 49ers fans with the type of trivia only a true fan will know. Each of the 13 chapters tests you on a specific topic, including the history of the team, specific position groups, and the 28 Hall-of-Famers who are somehow affiliated with the San Francisco 49ers. Each chapter is divided into 20 multiple-choice or true-false questions, the answers, then 10 facts about the topic that either add information about a certain question or shed light on a random part of the 49ers' history.

Do not be alarmed if some of these questions stump you, that is indeed the point of these questions. We hope you learn something new after devouring this book and use it to show off to your fellow 49ers fans. So sit back, relax, and enjoy the hours of fun this book provides.

CHAPTER 1:

ORIGINS & HISTORY

QUIZ TIME!

1. In which league did the San Francisco 49ers make their professional debut?

    a. Pacific Football League
    b. All-America Football Conference
    c. California Football Association
    d. National American Football League

2. How did the franchise earn its 49ers nickname?

    a. They were the 49th professional football team in the United States.
    b. First Asian immigrants to the Bay Area in 1749
    c. California Gold Rush of 1849
    d. The owner's favorite number was 7.

3. In which year did the San Francisco 49ers join the National Football League?

    a. 1946
    b. 1948

c. 1949

d. 1950

4. Which team did the 49ers beat for their first NFL victory?

   a. Chicago Bears

   b. Green Bay Packers

   c. Detroit Lions

   d. New York Giants

5. In which year did San Francisco qualify for the NFL playoffs for the first time?

   a. 1958

   b. 1963

   c. 1970

   d. 1971

6. Who was the first coach of the San Francisco 49ers?

   a. Louis Spadia

   b. Pappy Waldorf

   c. Lawrence Shaw

   d. Jess Hill

7. Where did the 49ers play before moving to Candlestick Park in 1971?

   a. Kezar Stadium

   b. Morabito Stadium

   c. San Francisco Coliseum

   d. Memorial Field

8. Founder Anthony J. Morabito died of a heart attack at a 49ers game in 1957.

a. True

b. False

9. When did the Morabito family sell the 49ers to the DeBartolo family?

   a. 1958

   b. 1964

   c. 1972

   d. 1977

10. Where were the DeBartolos based when they bought the team, turning this blue-collar, Rust-Belt city into a "49ers town," according to one columnist?

    a. Grand Rapids, Michigan

    b. Youngstown, Ohio

    c. Scranton, Pennsylvania

    d. Gary, Indiana

11. Current chairwoman Denise DeBartolo became the first woman ever to have her name engraved on the Stanley Cup.

    a. True

    b. False

12. How many times have the 49ers won the NFC West since the AFL-NFL merger in 1970?

    a. 20

    b. 23

    c. 18

    d. 29

13. In which season did San Francisco lead the NFL in both yards allowed and yards gained?

    a. 1984
    b. 1985
    c. 1987
    d. 1992

14. Which is the only current NFC team who has NEVER faced the 49ers in the postseason?

    a. Carolina Panthers
    b. New Orleans Saints
    c. Atlanta Falcons
    d. Arizona Cardinals

15. How many wins does San Francisco have in primetime games?

    a. 68
    b. 72
    c. 75
    d. 83

16. As expected, Jerry Rice has four of the top five marks for most receiving yards in a *Monday Night Football* game. Whose 286-yard performance in a Monday night game against the Rams is the only other person on the list?

    a. George Kittle
    b. Terrell Owens
    c. John Taylor
    d. J.J. Stoke

17. Who made history with the 49ers in Super Bowl LIV by becoming the first female coach in the NFL's championship game?

    a. Jennifer King
    b. Callie Brownson
    c. Lori Locust
    d. Katie Sowers

18. How many players have played at least 10 seasons for the 49ers?

    a. 39
    b. 46
    c. 51
    d. 64

19. How many members are there in the 49ers' Hall of Fame?

    a. 19
    b. 23
    c. 28
    d. 35

20. San Francisco has qualified for the playoffs after every Super Bowl in which it has played.

    a. True
    b. False

QUIZ ANSWERS

1. B – All-America Football Conference

2. C – California Gold Rush of 1849

3. D – 1950

4. C – Detroit Lions

5. C – 1970

6. C – Lawrence Shaw

7. A – Kezar Stadium

8. A – True

9. D – 1977

10. B – Youngstown, Ohio

11. B – False, She was the third.

12. A – 20

13. C – 1987

14. D – Arizona Cardinals

15. C – 75

16. C – John Taylor

17. D – Katie Sowers

18. C – 51

19. C – 28

20. B – False, They missed out in 1982.

DID YOU KNOW?

1. Anthony Morabito petitioned the NFL unsuccessfully for a team in San Francisco twice in the 1940s before he was awarded a franchise in the All-America Football Conference. In 1942, he made his first pitch to NFL officials, but it was a quick rejection from the league. Morabito tried again two years later in a meeting with commissioner Elmer Layden, but the league was hesitant to expand its footprint west of Chicago. It was after that meeting that Morabito was put in contact with Arch Ward, then the sports editor of the *Chicago Tribune*, who was looking to build the AAFC. The first meeting of the AAFC took place on June 6, 1944—also known as D-Day.

2. San Francisco was a powerhouse in its four years playing in the AAFC, but the 49ers never won the championship. They went 39-15-2, but were unfortunately in the same division as the Cleveland Browns, which won all four league titles and lost just four times. San Francisco actually handed the Browns two of those four losses, but the only time the 49ers even made it to the championship game was 1949 when the league scrapped divisions and had the top two teams play for the title.

3. Anthony Morabito was warned several times in the years preceding his death that the stresses of owning a football team and being involved in the day-to-day operations was

not good for his failing heart. In response to those concerns, he reportedly said, "What the hell, if I'm going to die, I might as well die at a football game." As if seeing his own future, Morabito died on October 27, 1957, while the 49ers were hosting the Chicago Bears at Kezar Stadium. As San Francisco lined up to kickoff after scoring a touchdown, Morabito collapsed and was administered his final absolution by Father Bill McGuire of St. James parish. The 49ers trailed 17-7 in the third quarter when they were told of their owner's death, and they rallied to beat the Bears 21-17 that day.

4. The 49ers have only been owned by two families in their 74-year history. After Anthony Morabito's death, his brother, Victor, ran the team until his death in 1964 after which their widows continued as owners, with Lou Spadia staying on as team president. The Morabitos sold the team in 1977 to Ed DeBartolo Sr., starting the next line of succession that has passed the 49ers to Ed DeBartolo Jr., then his sister, Denise DeBartolo York, and her husband, John York. The chain is likely to continue as Jed York, son of Denise and John York, is about to start his 11th season as the 49ers' CEO.

5. The DeBartolo/York family is very involved in professional sports across the world. At the same time as owning the 49ers, the DeBartolos also owned the NHL's Pittsburgh Penguins with daughter—and current 49ers chairwoman— Denise DeBartolo running the club as the team's president. Ed DeBartolo Sr. tried to purchase the Chicago White Sox in

1980, but his bid was not approved by enough American League owners. In May 2018, the Yorks and 49ers Enterprises purchased a 10% stake in Leeds United, which won promotion to the Premier League for the 2020-21 season.

6. The Yorks established the Edward J. DeBartolo Sr. 49ers Hall of Fame in 2009 to honor the legacy of the franchise. Most of the 28 people in the Hall of Fame were inducted in the inaugural class of 2009, which featured every player and coach who had either his jersey number retired or was inducted into the Pro Football Hall of Fame. In all, 17 people were part of that first class, and only Ed DeBartolo Jr. did not fit one of those two criteria. Founders Anthony and Victor Morabito even had to wait until 2010 to be inducted along with Jerry Rice, who had only retired five years earlier.

7. Candlestick Park holds the record for hosting the most *Monday Night Football* games since 1970, with 36 games. The final regular-season game at the historic stadium was the 36th and final time it was featured on Monday night, a 34-24 win over the Atlanta Falcons on December 23, 2013. San Francisco was 25-11 in those Monday night games and won their last five appearances on *Monday Night Football* at Candlestick Park.

8. The NFC West has continued to change as the NFL has expanded and grown since the 1970 merger. The one constant has been the Rams franchise, which have been in

the same division as the 49ers since 1950, even after they moved to St. Louis. San Francisco has a 71-67-3 record against their California-based rivals, including the 1989 NFC Championship game, the only time the two teams have ever met in the playoffs. San Francisco has a 19-17 record against the Arizona Cardinals and a 13-24 mark against the Seattle Seahawks since the current divisions were established in 2002.

9. When the 49ers make the playoffs, they have often made a lot of noise in the postseason. San Francisco has qualified for the playoffs 26 times, and has appeared in the NFC Championship Game 16 times with a 7-9 record. Those 16 appearances are tied with the Cowboys and Steelers for the most conference championship game appearances in the Super Bowl era.

10. Katie Sowers is an offensive assistant with the 49ers and became the first woman and first openly gay coach in the Super Bowl in 2020. She joined the franchise in 2017 as a seasonal assistant through the Bill Walsh Minority Fellowship and worked with the team's wide receivers. She played eight seasons in the Women's Football Alliance and was part of the 2013 United States national team that won a gold medal at the Women's World Championships.

CHAPTER 2:

NUMBERS GAME

QUIZ TIME!

1. How many defensive players have their number retired by the San Francisco 49ers?

    a. 9

    b. 2

    c. 6

    d. 3

2. How many jerseys have the 49ers retired since last winning the Super Bowl?

    a. 2

    b. 3

    c. 4

    d. 5

3. Which quarterback brought John Brodie's number 12 out of retirement for his two-year stint with the 49ers?

    a. Shaun Hill

    b. Trent Dilfer

c. Elvis Grbac

d. Tim Rattay

4. Which player NEVER wore number 1 for the 49ers?

   a. Gary Andersen

   b. Troy Smith

   c. Jose Cortez

   d. David Akers

5. The last player to wear number 7 for San Francisco was Colin Kaepernick.

   a. True

   b. False

6. Which of the following players has had his jersey retired by the 49ers and is enshrined in the Pro Football Hall of Fame?

   a. Dwight Clark

   b. Hugh McElhenny

   c. John Brodie

   d. Charlie Krueger

7. Who was the first player to wear number 8 for the San Francisco 49ers?

   a. Max Runager

   b. Steve Young

   c. Larry Wilson

   d. Tom Orosz

8. Since Terrell Owens left the 49ers in 2003, how many years has no one worn the number 81?

a. 2

b. 4

c. 6

d. 8

9. Which Super Bowl champion quarterback wore the number 16 for San Francisco for two seasons prior to Joe Montana's arrival in 1979?

a. Len Dawson

b. Ken Stabler

c. Fran Tarkenton

d. Jim Plunkett

10. Charles Haley wore number 94 for every game he ever played for the San Francisco 49ers.

a. True

b. False

11. University of Minnesota football coach P.J. Fleck played for San Francisco in 2004 in what was the only NFL game in his career. Which current 49ers player now wears the number he wore that day?

a. Jimmy Garoppolo

b. Deebo Samuels

c. George Kittle

d. Mitch Wishnowsky

12. Jerry Rice was the last player to wear number 80 for the 49ers, but eight players wore it before Rice made it famous for 15 seasons. Who was the last player to wear the number prior to Rice's arrival in 1985?

a. Russ Francis

b. Terry LeCount

c. Eason Ramson

d. Charles Smith

13. What number did long-time left tackle Joe Staley wear?

a. 68

b. 71

c. 72

d. 74

14. Which player whose number has been retired by the 49ers had the longest tenure in San Francisco?

a. Joe Montana

b. John Brodie

c. Jerry Rice

d. Dwight Clark

15. Isaac Bruce made the number 80 famous in St. Louis, but he had to choose a new number when he finished his career with the 49ers. Which number did he wear during his two seasons with San Francisco?

a. 18

b. 81

c. 88

d. 84

16. Running back Frank Gore started his long career of 10 seasons with the 49ers and ran for more than 11,000 yards with the team. What number did he wear while bulldozing over defenders out in the backfield?

a. 27

b. 24

c. 20

d. 21

17. Despite the fact Patrick Willis retired six years ago, no one else has worn his number 52 since he left.

    a. True

    b. False

18. How many players have worn the number 49 for the 49ers?

    a. 8

    b. 13

    c. 18

    d. 26

19. Which player has worn the most different uniform numbers for the 49ers?

    a. Del Rodgers

    b. Visco Grgich

    c. Ed Henke

    d. Don Burke

20. If C.J. Beathard makes the 2020 roster, he would become the 49ers player who has worn the number 3 the longest.

    a. True

    b. False

QUIZ ANSWERS

1. D – 3

2. D – 5

3. B – Trent Dilfer

4. D – David Akers

5. A – True

6. B – Hugh McElhenny

7. B – Steve Young

8. B – 4

9. D – Jim Plunkett

10. B – False

11. A – Jimmy Garoppolo

12. C – Eason Ramson

13. D – 74

14. B – John Brodie

15. C – 88

16. D – 21

17. A – True

18. B – 13

19. D – Don Burke (5 different numbers)

20. A – True

DID YOU KNOW?

six

1. The 49ers have retired 12 numbers in
    cover a wide swath of the team's history. Half of those
    whose numbers have been retired dressed for San
    Francisco at some time in 1950s, and Jerry Rice is the only
    player who wore the 49ers jersey in the 2000s. The team
    has retired the numbers of three quarterbacks, two
    running backs, two offensive linemen, two wide receivers,
    two defensive backs, and one defensive lineman.

2. Steve Young almost never wore number 8 for the 49ers. If
    he had gotten his way, he would have worn the number 14
    throughout his entire career. However, that number was
    taken when he arrived as a freshman at Brigham Young,
    and he was given 8 instead. That was the number he wore
    for the rest of his career, and now he's the only 49ers
    player that will ever wear that number.

3. Four of the 49ers' retired jerseys were worn by other
    players after the honoree left the franchise. Kermit
    Alexander wore Hugh McElhenny's 39 from 1963-69
    before the number was finally retired by the team in 1971.
    Two players wore number 73 after Leo Nomellini retired
    in 1963, but Dave McCormick lasted just one season with
    the team, and Lance Olssen lasted two in San Francisco
    before the number was taken out of circulation in '71. Bob
    St. Clair was the first 49ers player to wear number 79, and

19

others wore it after him before the team retired the number in 2001.

4. Trent Dilfer and John Brodie were very good friends and golfing partners, which is why Dilfer felt comfortable enough to ask Brodie for his permission to wear number 12 for the 49ers. They met through former NFL quarterback Chris Chandler, who is Brodie's son-in-law and a good friend of Dilfer's from the quarterback fraternity. Dilfer wanted to wear number 12 to mostly honor Brodie, who he considered a hero, but he also was hopeful it would shine a light on Brodie's career and lead to his induction in the Pro Football Hall of Fame.

5. There is plenty of debate around whether or not the 49ers should retire Terrell Owens's number 81. After an eight-year career with the team that launched his now Hall-of-Fame career, many believe Owens deserves to have his number retired by the team. However, San Francisco has been willing to hand out his number in the 16 seasons since Owens left the team. In total, 12 different players have worn the uniform since Owens was traded to the Ravens, then to Philadelphia in March 2004.

6. Charles Haley is the only Hall-of-Famer to wear number 94, but that wasn't the number he wore for his entire career. Haley was lured out of retirement by San Francisco for the 1998 playoffs after he didn't play in the 1997 or 1998 regular season. The number 94 was taken by defensive tackle David Richie at the time, so Haley wore

number 95 for his two playoff games. When Haley was re-signed for the 1999 season, he was reunited with his number 94 uniform.

7. Frankie Albert wore number 63 as the first quarterback for the San Francisco 49ers, which is the highest jersey number worn by a quarterback in the franchise's NFL history. However, Bev Wallace wore number 64 as Albert's backup from 1947-49. Albert eventually changed his number to 13 for the 1952 season.

8. Don Burke wore five different numbers during his five years with the franchise: 32, 38, 66, 68, and 73. His teammate, Visco Grgich, wore four numbers in seven seasons with the team from 1946-52. There are a handful of players who wore three different jersey numbers for the 49ers, including Max McCaffrey, who was credited with three different numbers in his one season with the team.

9. Oddly, no player has ever worn number 1 for more than one season with San Francisco, but Shawn Poindexter might become the first if he can make the 2020 roster out of training camp. The number is usually worn by a specialist, but only two kickers have worn it for the 49ers—Gary Andersen in 1997 and Jose Cortez in 2005. It's been worn three times by wide receivers, including Poindexter.

10. In July 2020, CBS Sports released a list of the greatest NFL players to wear each of the 99 jersey numbers. In total, 12 different players on the list played for the 49ers, but only 6 spent more than two seasons with the franchise. Those six

honorees on the list were Steve Young (8), Joe Montana (16), Jimmy Johnson (37), Ronnie Lott (42), Tim McDonald (46), and Jerry Rice (80). Former San Francisco head coach Mike Singletary was chosen as the representative for number 50.

CHAPTER 3:

HAIL TO ALMA MATER

QUIZ TIME!

1. John Brodie is the longest-tenured 49ers player in franchise history, and he didn't have to go far after being drafted by the team in 1957. At which school did Brodie attend and play football?

    a. California

    b. Stanford

    c. Fresno State

    d. Redlands College

2. The 49ers have drafted 1st overall three times in their history. Which school did NOT produce one of those three number 1 picks?

    a. Texas Tech

    b. Georgia

    c. Alabama

    d. Utah

    e.

3. John Taylor is the most successful professional football player to come out of which MEAC program?

    a. Delaware State
    b. North Carolina Central
    c. Norfolk State
    d. Howard

4. Where did Jimmy Garoppolo play college football?

    a. Southern Illinois
    b. Illinois State
    c. Eastern Illinois
    d. Western Illinois

5. Richard Sherman came to Stanford as a wide receiver, but transitioned to cornerback before ever appearing in a game on offense.

    a. True
    b. False

6. From where did Hall of Fame 49ers coach Bill Walsh graduate after an injury-plagued college playing career?

    a. UCLA
    b. Fresno State
    c. San Jose State
    d. Oregon State

7. Before going on to become a successful NFL coach, former 49ers head coach George Seifert coached two seasons at which Ivy League school?

a. Cornell
b. Harvard
c. Princeton
d. Yale

8. Charles Haley is the only player in the Pro Football Hall of Fame from which school in Virginia?

a. Randolph-Macon
b. Virginia Tech
c. James Madison
d. William & Mary

9. The 49ers have drafted only two players from a non-Power Five school in the 1st round since selecting Jerry Rice in 1985. One of those players is defensive back Jimmie Ward, who San Francisco drafted 30th overall in 2014 out of which MAC school?

a. Akron
b. Kent State
c. Western Michigan
d. Northern Illinois

10. Ward and fellow defensive back Dontae Johnson are now the longest-tenured 49ers who were drafted by the team. Johnson was selected from which ACC school in the 3rd round of the 2014 NFL Draft?

a. North Carolina State
b. North Carolina
c. Duke
d. Wake Forest

11. Nick Mullens started half of the 49ers' games in 2018 after Jimmy Garoppolo and C.J. Beathard both went down with injuries. Where did Mullens play college football before going undrafted in the 2017 NFL Draft?

    a. Mississippi State
    b. Southern Mississippi
    c. Louisiana Tech
    d. Arkansas State

12. Which 49ers running back left college early after rushing for a school-record 2,036 yards as a junior?

    a. Tom Rathman
    b. Raheem Mostert
    c. Tevin Coleman
    d. Frank Gore

13. Notre Dame and Southern California are tied for the most Hall-of-Famers with 13 from each school. Which school produced more Hall-of-Famers who played for the 49ers?

    a. Notre Dame
    b. Southern California
    c. Tie
    d. No 49ers player inducted into the Hall has played for either school.

14. Andy Lee set most of the 49ers' records for single-season and career punting during his 11-year stint with the team from 2004 to 2014. At which school did Lee ply his trade before being drafted by San Francisco in the 6th round?

a. Penn State

b. Pittsburgh

c. Rutgers

d. Utah

15. Tramaine Brock went from an undrafted free agent in 2010 to a starter for the 49ers in 2015. At which then-NAIA school did Brock play his senior year of college?

a. Belhaven University

b. Berea College

c. Bob Jones University

d. Berry College

16. The 49ers' first coach, Lawrence Shaw, played for legendary Notre Dame coach Knute Rockne and was part of the his first two Fighting Irish teams that finished unbeaten.

a. True

b. False

17. Heading into training camp in 2020, two schools are tied with three players each on the 49ers' roster. Which two schools are tied on the list?

a. Wisconsin and USC

b. Iowa and Tennessee

c. Stanford and Michigan

d. Alabama and LSU

18. How many non-FBS or FCS players were on the 49ers' roster when they went to the Super Bowl after the 2012 season?

a. 1

b. 2

c. 3

d. 4

19. As a rookie in 2017, tight end George Kittle had as many catches with the 49ers as he had in four years at Iowa.

    a. True

    b. False

20. Where did 49ers defensive coordinator Robert Saleh play tight end for four years in college?

    a. Northern Michigan

    b. Lake Superior State

    c. Minnesota-Mankato

    d. Butte Junior College

QUIZ ANSWERS

1. B – Stanford

2. C – Alabama

3. A – Delaware State

4. C – Eastern Illinois

5. B – False

6. C – San Jose State

7. A – Cornell

8. C – James Madison

9. D – Northern Illinois

10. A – North Carolina State

11. B – Southern Mississippi

12. C – Tevin Coleman

13. C – Tie (Both have had 2.)

14. B – Pittsburgh

15. A – Belhaven University

16. A – True

17. B – Iowa and Tennessee

18. C – 3

19. B – False

20. A – Northern Michigan

DID YOU KNOW?

1. Nick Mullens threw for nearly 12,000 yards in his career at Southern Mississippi, but struggled to find a footing in the NFL. He was signed as an undrafted free agent by the 49ers in May 2017, but was cut in September right after the final preseason game. He was re-signed at the end of the 2017 season, but was cut again as one of the last casualties of the preseason. Mullens returned to the 49ers' practice squad for three weeks before being promoted to the active roster for the first time after Jimmy Garoppolo tore his ACL.

2. Jimmie Ward was a critical member of the 2012 and 2013 Northern Illinois Huskies that went 24-4 and skyrocketed the program to national prominence with 15 combined weeks inside the top 25 polls. Ward was a semifinalist for the Jim Thorpe Award as a senior in 2013, the same year he was named a First Team All-American by *Sports Illustrated* and *USA Today* and to the All-American Third Team by the Associated Press and Athlon Sports.

3. Richard Sherman came to Stanford as a decorated wide receiver prospect and made an instant impact by leading the Cardinals in receiving his first two seasons. However, a partial tear in his left patellar tendon early in his junior year sidelined him for the season, and he returned to the field as a defensive back. He intercepted six passes in 26

games as a cornerback for Stanford to become the shutdown corner he is today.

4. Tramaine Brock played at three different schools before battling his way into the NFL. He played his first two seasons of college football at Mississippi Gulf Coast Community College, helping the program win the national championship as a sophomore in 2007. He transferred to the University of Minnesota in 2008 and started 13 games at safety for the Golden Gophers, finishing the season with 73 tackles, an interception, and three forced fumbles. After becoming academically ineligible before the 2009 season, Brock played his final year at Belhaven and had six interceptions and 10 passes defended to go along with 51 tackles and 2.5 sacks.

5. The 49ers struck gold when it comes to receivers from the Football Championship Subdivision—the former Division I-AA—in the 1980s and '90s. San Francisco obviously plucked Jerry Rice from Mississippi Valley State with the 16th overall pick in 1985, but the following year, they drafted John Taylor out of Delaware State in the 3rd round. The duo became the top weapons of the 49ers' passing attack after Dwight Clark's retirement in 1987. When Taylor retired after the 1995 season, he was replaced by Terrell Owens, a 1996 3rd round pick out of Tennessee-Chattanooga. Owens went on to finish second behind Rice in most of the franchise's career receiving categories in his eight years with the team.

6. The 2020 49ers currently have plenty of sets of college teammates on the roster, but it's unique to have three players who were all college teammates. That's the case for the trio of Tennessee Volunteers on the San Francisco roster. Cornerback Emmanuel Moseley, defensive lineman Jonathan Kongbo, and rookie wideout Jauan Jennings all played together for Tennessee during the 2016 and 2017 seasons before Moseley graduated. Kongbo left the school after the 2018 season, and Jennings was drafted in the 7th round of the 2020 NFL Draft.

7. Perhaps none of the sets of college teammates on the 49ers are as close as C.J. Beathard and George Kittle. The duo has now been teammates for the last eight seasons, starting when both were freshmen at Iowa in 2013 through the first four years of their professional career. In their last two years with the Hawkeyes, the two connected 42 times for 604 yards and 10 touchdowns in 25 games.

8. Notre Dame and Southern California became rivals on the gridiron because of their success in the college football landscape over the last century. Both schools have 13 alums enshrined in the Pro Football Hall of Fame, and two from each school suited up for the 49ers. Joe Montana is the quintessential Notre Dame alum who played for San Francisco, but the school also claims former owner Ed DeBartolo Jr. Ronnie Lott represents USC and the 49ers in Canton, Ohio, but O.J. Simpson played a season in San Francisco as well in his career.

9. Bob St. Clair basically played his entire football career on the same city block. The San Francisco native played high school football across the street from the 49ers' home at Kezar Stadium, then played his first two college football seasons at the University of San Francisco. When the Dons dropped football after a perfect 9-0 season, he transferred to the University of Tulsa until getting drafted by the hometown 49ers. The 1951 USF football team had nine players enter the pros, and three ended up in the Pro Football Hall of Fame.

10. Two 49ers players won a national championship during their college football career, though neither one contributed much in those victories. Rookie defensive back Jared Mayden appeared in seven games during Alabama's national championship season in 2017, recording four tackles in his appearances. Dee Ford had 11 tackles and two sacks in 2010 when Auburn won the national championship.

CHAPTER 4:

CALLING THE SIGNALS

QUIZ TIME!

1. Who was the first 49ers quarterback to throw for more than 2,000 yards in a season?

    a. Y.A. Tittle
    b. Frankie Albert
    c. Joe Montana
    d. John Brodie

2. Jimmy Garoppolo wasted no time acclimating to San Francisco after being traded from New England. How many straight starts did Garoppolo win to start his 49ers career?

    e. 4
    f. 5
    g. 6
    h. 7

3. John Brodie had more losses as the 49ers' starting quarterback than Alex Smith had starts as the 49ers' quarterback.

a. True

b. False

4. How many Heisman Trophy winners have started a game for the 49ers at quarterback?

   a. 3
   b. 4
   c. 5
   d. 6

5. Which quarterback who started just one game for the 49ers lost that game?

   a. Ty Detmer
   b. Chris Weinke
   c. Jim Druckenmiller
   d. Mike Moroski

6. How many touchdowns did Nick Mullens throw in 2018 during his eight-game run as the 49ers' starter?

   a. 9
   b. 11
   c. 13
   d. 15

7. What is the highest completion percentage Joe Montana ever had in a game in which he threw at least 10 passes for the 49ers?

   a. 81.6
   b. 82.7
   c. 83.9
   d. 84.4

8. Which quarterback who has made at least 25 starts for the 49ers has the best winning percentage?

   a. Joe Montana
   b. Jimmy Garoppolo
   c. Steve Young
   d. John Brodie

9. Who laid the hit on Steve Young in 1999 that ultimately ended his Hall of Fame career?

   a. Corey Chavous
   b. Simeon Rice
   c. Tommy Bennett
   d. Aeneas Williams

10. In which season did Jeff Garcia lead the NFC in completions and passing yards while setting the 49ers' single-season record in those stats in the process?

   a. 2000
   b. 2001
   c. 2002
   d. 2003

11. Joe Montana and Steve Young account for more than half of the 300-yard passing games in San Francisco's history.

   a. True
   b. False

12. In how many seasons did Joe Montana start every game the 49ers played?

a. 3

b. 4

c. 5

d. 6

13. Joe Montana is the only San Francisco quarterback to throw for 450 yards in a game.

a. True

b. False

14. In how many seasons did the 49ers have a losing record in games Steve Young started?

a. 0

b. 1

c. 2

d. 3

15. Steve Young was known for his ability to run as well as he threw the ball, rushing for 4,239 yards in his NFL career. How many rushing touchdowns did he have with San Francisco?

a. 29

b. 33

c. 37

d. 43

16. Who is the only San Francisco quarterback to throw for a touchdown in 18 consecutive games without missing one during the streak?

a. Joe Montana

b. Alex Smith

c. Steve Young

d. Colin Kaepernick

17. Who holds the 49ers' record for the most completions in a game?

    a. Joe Montana

    b. Steve Young

    c. Tim Rattay

    d. Jeff Garcia

18. Jeff Garcia had a winning record as a starting quarterback for the 49ers.

    a. True

    b. False

19. In which season was San Francisco NOT forced to start four different quarterbacks?

    a. 1974

    b. 1999

    c. 2005

    d. 2007

20. Tim Rattay set the record for fewest passing yards in a season in 2000 when his only pass of the season was completed for -4 yards. Against whom did Rattay throw this fateful pass to Fred Beasley?

    a. Green Bay Packers

    b. St. Louis Rams

    c. San Diego Chargers

    d. Oakland Raiders

QUIZ ANSWERS

1. A – Y.A. Tittle

2. B – 5

3. A – True

4. C – 5

5. B – Chris Weinke

6. C – 13

7. D – 84.4

8. C – Steve Young

9. D – Aeneas Williams

10. A – 2000

11. B – False

12. A – 3

13. B – False

14. B – 1

15. C – 37

16. D – Colin Kaepernick

17. C – Tim Rattay

18. B – False

19. B – 1999

20. C – San Diego Chargers

DID YOU KNOW?

1. Jimmy Garoppolo is one of five quarterbacks to win their first seven starts in the NFL, and the first to do so since Ben Roethlisberger won his first 15 in 2004. He became the first 49ers quarterback to ever win his first five starts by leading San Francisco to five straight victories to close the 2017 season. He set a team record by throwing for 1,542 yards in those five starts, the most any San Francisco quarterback has thrown in his first five starts with the team.

2. The five Heisman Trophy winners who started at least one game at quarterback for San Francisco had mixed results for the franchise. They combined for a 28-31-1 record with the team over parts of 10 different seasons. The last Heisman winner to start for San Francisco was Troy Smith, who went 3-3 for the 49ers in 2010.

3. The first was Steve Spurrier, who went on to be one of the best college football coaches of the last 30 years. Spurrier played in 92 games over nine seasons with the team, throwing 5,250 yards and 33 touchdowns despite tossing 48 interceptions and only completing 52.5% of his passes. His best season came in 1972 when he won six of nine starts and threw for 1,983 yards and 18 touchdowns, both the most in his career. It was also that season when he had arguably his best game as a pro by tying the team record at

the time with five touchdown tosses in a 34-21 win over the Bears on November 19.

4. John Brodie found a second career as a professional golfer on the PGA's Champions Tour after retiring from the NFL in 1973. He qualified for the U.S. Open at Winged Foot in 1959 and missed the cut by three strokes. He also played in the 1981 U.S. Open at Merion, but once again missed the cut, this time by 15 shots. He made the cut in 227 of the 230 Champions Tour events he played and made more than $735,000 in his golf career. He finished in the top ten 12 times, was the runner-up of two tournaments, and hit a pinnacle by winning the 1991 Security Pacific Senior Classic.

5. Joe Montana created an aura around the 49ers with his ability to orchestrate game-winning drives in the fourth quarter. It became known as "Montana Magic" with 31 fourth-quarter comebacks for San Francisco. The pinnacle came in Super Bowl XXIII when Montana led a 92-yard drive in the final 3:20 against the Bengals, capped off by a 10-yard touchdown to John Taylor to win the game 20-16. It was the third of Montana's four Super Bowl victories and the only one in which he was not named MVP.

6. Y.A. Tittle was the sole starting quarterback for the 49ers in just one of his 10 seasons with the team from 1951-60. The Hall-of-Famer had just one losing season as San Francisco's starter and remains fifth on the team in passing yards, passing attempts, and touchdowns. As the 49ers

switched to a shotgun formation under Red Hickey, they traded Tittle to the Giants, where he blossomed in four seasons. Tittle led the Giants to three straight Eastern Division titles, but lost in the championship all three years—in 1961 and 1962 to Green Bay and in 1963 to Chicago. He threw for a league-high 33 touchdowns in 1962, then set a record the following season with 36 touchdowns.

7. Between 1980 and 1997, San Francisco led the NFL in completion percentage 10 times as Joe Montana and Steve Young both led the league five times. Young won the title four straight seasons from 1994-97, the second-longest streak in NFL history. Young also is tied with Sammy Baugh for most seasons leading the league in passer rating with six times, all of which came within a seven-year span from 1991-97 for Young.

8. Jeff Garcia was a four-time All-Star in the Canadian Football League in five seasons with the Calgary Stampeders. In a 2017 interview, Garcia admitted he wasn't expecting the NFL to call by the time he led Calgary to the Grey Cup in 1998 as the MVP of the game. However, he was signed as Steve Young's backup for the 1999 season, and when Young was concussed by Aeneas Williams, Garcia took the reins. The following year, he set the franchise record for most completions (355) and passing yards (4,278) in a season and became the team's starter until the end of the 2003 season.

9. C.J. Beathard comes from a famous football family as the grandson of former Washington and San Diego general manager Bobby Beathard. He set the 49ers franchise record for longest touchdown pass by a rookie with an 83-yard scoring pass to Marquise Goodwin on November 12, 2017, against the Giants. He added a 47-yard strike to Garrett Celek in the game to become the first San Francisco rookie to throw two touchdowns of 45 yards or more.

10. Colin Kaepernick made a name for himself more for his actions off the field than what he did on it. Kaepernick was one of the first professional athletes to draw attention to racial injustice in the United States by kneeling during the playing of the national anthem. The backlash and media firestorm that ensued made Kaepernick a toxic figure in the eyes of many NFL teams despite his talent. He last played in the NFL in 2016 and went unsigned when he tested the free agency market after that season. He filed a lawsuit against the league for collusion in October 2017, which was resolved in February 2019. Kaepernick had a publicized workout in November 2019 that was sponsored by the NFL, but changed the plans at the last minute due to issues with the conditions set upon him by the league.

CHAPTER 5:

BETWEEN THE TACKLES

QUIZ TIME!

1. Frank Gore has played the most games at running back for the 49ers at 148 contests. Who ranks second?

   a. Roger Craig

   b. Joe Perry

   c. Tom Rathman

   d. Hugh McElhenny

2. How many rushing attempts did Frank Gore have with the 49ers?

   a. 2,442

   b. 1,908

   c. 2,598

   d. 3,125

3. The 49ers' record for most rushing touchdowns in a season is 10. Which player does NOT share that record?

   a. Frank Gore

   b. Ricky Watters

c. Joe Perry

d. Garrison Hearst

4. Who was the starting halfback for the 49ers in their first Super Bowl appearance?

   a. Roger Craig

   b. Ricky Patton

   c. Johnny Davis

   d. Bill Ring

5. In which year did Frank Gore set the franchise record for rushing yards in a season?

   a. 2004

   b. 2005

   c. 2006

   d. 2007

6. The playoff single-game rushing record Raheem Mostert broke in the NFC Championship Game after the 2019 season was held by a running back.

   a. True

   b. False

7. Which running back has NEVER run for 1,500 yards in a season for San Francisco?

   a. Garrison Hearst

   b. Frank Gore

   c. Charlie Garner

   d. Roger Craig

8. From 2006 to 2014, Frank Gore ran for at least 1,000 yards in every season except one. How many yards did he rush for in 2010?

   a. 794
   b. 853
   c. 914
   d. 972

9. Garrison Hearst was named an All-Pro running back by the Associated Press during his 49ers career.

   a. True
   b. False

10. How many rushing attempts did Raheem Mostert have before bursting onto the scene in 2019 as part of San Francisco's backfield.

    a. 41
    b. 46
    c. 53
    d. 62

11. Garrison Hearst holds the record for the longest rush in San Francisco. How long was his 1998 run against the Jets that set the record?.

    a. 99
    b. 98
    c. 97
    d. 96

12. Which running back never shared a backfield with Frank Gore during his 49ers career?

    a. Shaun Draughn
    b. Brian Westbrook
    c. Carlos Hyde
    d. Kevan Barlow

13. Which 49ers running back ranks third in franchise history in receptions?

    a. Paul Hofer
    b. Frank Gore
    c. Roger Craig
    d. Tom Rathman

14. Who is the only San Francisco running back in the top 15 of the franchise's rushing yards list who didn't average at least four yards per carry?

    a. Frank Gore
    b. Ken Willard
    c. Joe Perry
    d. Wilbur Jackson

15. Fullback Tom Rathman had more 100-yard receiving games in his 49ers career than 100-yard rushing games.

    a. True
    b. False

16. How many 100-yard rushing games did Wendell Tyler have in 1984 when he ran for a then-record 1,262 yards?

a. 3

b. 4

c. 5

d. 6

17. Against whom did Charlie Garner become the first 49ers running back to run for 200 yards in a game?

    a. St. Louis Rams

    b. Dallas Cowboys

    c. New York Giants

    d. Atlanta Falcons

18. Hall-of-Famer Joe Perry was the first player in NFL history to rush for 1,000 yards in a single season. In which two years did he accomplish the feat?

    a. 1951-52

    b. 1948-49

    c. 1958-59

    d. 1953-54

19. As a rookie in 1952, Hugh McElhenny set the 49ers' record for highest rushing average. How many yards did he average on his 98 carries that season?

    a. 6.43

    b. 6.87

    c. 6.98

    d. 7.12

20. Which 49ers running back was the first to score four total touchdowns in a regular-season game?

a. Tevin Coleman
b. Frank Gore
c. Roger Craig
d. Joe Perry

QUIZ ANSWERS

1. B – Joe Perry

2. A – 2,442

3. D – Garrison Hearst

4. B – Ricky Patton

5. C – 2006

6. B – False

7. C – Charlie Garner

8. B – 853

9. B – False

10. A – 41

11. D – 96

12. A – Shaun Draughn

13. C – Roger Craig

14. B – Ken Willard

15. A – True

16. B – 4

17. B – Dallas Cowboys

18. D – 1953-54

19. C – 6.98

20. A – Tevin Coleman

DID YOU KNOW?

1. Raheem Mostert was the breakout star of 2019 for the 49ers as he burst onto the scene as the team's leading rusher. He had a tumultuous journey to San Francisco. He was signed by six teams in a little more than a year as mostly a practice squad body or special teams ace. He didn't get his first NFL carry until the final game of the 2016 season when he ran for six yards against Seattle. He had his first career 100-yard game against Baltimore on December 1, 2019, then became a household name with his 220 yards and four touchdowns against Green Bay in the NFC Championship game.

2. Hugh McElhenny and Joe Perry were teammates for nine seasons, and they are the two running backs enshrined in the Hall of Fame who spent more than two seasons with the 49ers. Perry ran for 5,922 yards while teammates with McElhenny from 1952-60, and McElhenny ran for 4,288 yards in his San Francisco career. Both players left the team after the 1960 season, but Perry came back in 1963 and retired with the 49ers after running for 98 yards on 24 carries in nine games that same year.

3. Joe Perry is the only 49ers player in the Hall of Fame with any ties to the franchise's pre-NFL roots. He was spotted by a 49ers player while playing football for his Alameda, California, navy base's team, and that unnamed player

reported back to ownership. San Francisco offered Perry a contract that he accepted after completing his military service in 1948. Perry ran for more than 1,300 yards and scored 23 total touchdowns in his two seasons playing in the AAFC.

4. Two other Hall of Fame running backs suited up for the 49ers during their careers. John Henry Johnson began his career in San Francisco and ran for 1,051 yards and 12 touchdowns in three seasons with the team. O.J. Simpson ended his Hall of Fame career with the 49ers and ran for 1,053 yards and four touchdowns in two seasons with the team.

5. Roger Craig had a historic season in 1985 when he became the first player to ever gain 1,000 rushing yards and 1,000 receiving yards in the same season. He scored nine rushing touchdowns and averaged 4.9 yards per carry, and also caught six touchdowns and averaged 11 yards per reception. He led the 49ers in rushing five straight times starting in 1985 and led them in catches four times with three of those seasons—1985, 1987, and 1988—overlapping.

6. Frank Gore passed Barry Sanders for third place on the NFL's career rushing list in 2019, and the 37-year-old continues to grind along in his career. It began with more than 11,000 yards in 10 seasons with the 49ers, rewriting the record book in the process. He's the team's career and single-season leader in rushing yards, rushing attempts, and rushing touchdowns in addition to most career 100-

yard games and most 100-yard performances in a single-season. He trails only Jerry Rice on the career list of yards from scrimmage.

7. Tevin Coleman's life has been a bit of a miracle. He was born 10 weeks premature and weighed just 3.5 pounds, and doctors gave him just a 20% chance to survive. But he defied the odds and continued to grow stronger, earning himself the nickname "Rock." Coleman was tough to stop in the Big Ten in his final two years at Indiana, averaging a little less than 7.5 yards per carry in 2013 and 2014. He was the Hoosiers' third unanimous consensus All-American in 2014 and finished 7th in Heisman Trophy voting after rushing for 2,036 yards and 15 touchdowns as a junior.

8. Tom Rathman won two Super Bowls in eight seasons with the 49ers as the team's fullback. He ran 506 times for 1,902 yards in 115 regular-season games, but he proved more useful as a receiver. He is 14th on the team's career receiving list with 294 career catches for 2,490 yards and eight scores. Rathman returned to San Francisco as the running backs coach for two separate stints. He served in the role from 1997-2002, then again from 2009-16.

9. Jeff Wilson Jr. is an accomplished drummer and played backup for his father, Jeff Sr., in a gospel singing group. Growing up 10 miles away from Adrian Peterson's hometown in Texas, Wilson would attend Peterson's high school games and try to emulate his running style in his youth football practices. Wilson scored four touchdowns

on 27 rushes and added three catches for a touchdown in 2019.

10. The 49ers have led the NFL in rushing three times in the Super Bowl era (1987, 1998, and 1999), but have never had the league's leading rusher. In 1987, Roger Craig's 815 yards ranked 8th in the league, the same ranking Charlie Garner had in 1999 when he ran for 1,229 yards. Garrison Hearst's 1,570 yards in 1998 was 3rd in the league, which is tied for the highest finish for a 49ers player. Frank Gore is the only 49ers running back to lead the NFC in rushing, which he accomplished in 2006 when he ran for 1,695 yards, but that also only ranked him 3rd in the NFL

CHAPTER 6:

CATCHING THE BALL

QUIZ TIME!

1. Which 49ers tight end holds the record for most receiving yards in a season for a tight end?

   a. George Kittle
   b. Vernon Davis
   c. Brent Jones
   d. Russ Francis

2. How many times did Jerry Rice catch three touchdowns in a playoff game?

   a. 0
   b. 1
   c. 2
   d. 3

3. Jerry Rice and Terrell Owens are the only wide receivers in the Pro Football Hall of Fame who played for the 49ers.

   a. True
   b. False

4. Who ranks 2nd in 49ers history in career playoff receiving yards?

   a. John Taylor
   b. Roger Craig
   c. Brent Jones
   d. Gene Washington

5. Who was on the receiving end of the longest pass in 49ers history?

   a. Jerry Rice
   b. John Taylor
   c. Terrell Owens
   d. Brandon Lloyd

6. How many times has the 49ers had two 1,000-yard receivers on the same team?

   a. 2
   b. 3
   c. 4
   d. 5

7. Which of these players NEVER finished 2nd in receiving yards behind Jerry Rice in multiple seasons?

   a. Roger Craig
   b. Terrell Owens
   c. Dwight Clark
   d. John Taylor

8. How far off the ground are Dwight Clark's feet on the statue depicting his famous catch outside Levi's Stadium?

a. 5 feet

b. 7 feet

c. 9 feet

d. 11 feet

9. In which season did Dwight Clark lead the NFL in receptions with 60?

a. 1980

b. 1981

c. 1982

d. 1983

10. Which 49ers player leads the franchise in punt returns and is 14 yards shy of leading San Francisco in punt return yards?

a. Ted Ginn Jr.

b. Dana McElmore

c. John Taylor

d. Kermit Alexander

11. Who was the first 49ers player to have 1,000 receiving yards in a season?

a. R.C. Owens

b. Billy Wilson

c. Dave Parks

d. Bernie Casey

12. Jerry Rice might not have gone over 1,000 yards receiving as a rookie in 1985, but he did catch 50 passes.

a. True

b. False

13. How many consecutive seasons did Jerry Rice eclipse 1,000 yards receiving?

    a. 8
    b. 9
    c. 10
    d. 11

14. In which season did Jerry Rice miss the only games of his career due to injury?

    a. 1995
    b. 1996
    c. 1997
    d. 1998

15. What was the fewest number of receptions Jerry Rice had in a season in which he had 1,000 yards receiving?

    a. 64
    b. 65
    c. 66
    d. 67

16. What was the most receiving yards Vernon Davis had in a season with San Francisco?

    a. 965
    b. 942
    c. 914
    d. 996

17. What was Vernon Davis's career high for touchdown catches?

a. 11
b. 12
c. 13
d. 14

18. Vernon Davis was San Francisco's leading receiver in the postseason in 2012-13 when the 49ers went to the Super Bowl.

    a. True
    b. False

19. Which of these 49ers single-game records does Terrell Owens hold?

    a. Most yards
    b. Most receptions
    c. Most touchdowns
    d. Best receiving average

20. Against which NFC West rival did Terrell Owens pull out a Sharpie and sign the football after scoring a touchdown on *Monday Night Football*?

    a. Arizona Cardinals
    b. St. Louis Rams
    c. New Orleans Saints
    d. Seattle Seahawks

QUIZ ANSWERS

1. A – George Kittle

2. D – 3

3. B – False

4. C – Brent Jones

5. B – John Taylor

6. B – 3

7. C – Dwight Clark

8. D – 11 feet

9. C – 1982

10. C – John Taylor

11. A – R.C. Owens

12. B – False

13. D – 11

14. C – 1997

15. A – 64

16. A – 965

17. C – 13

18. B – False

19. B – Most receptions

20. D – Settle Seahawks

DID YOU KNOW?

1. Much is talked about the seasons when Jerry Rice was perfectly healthy, but the 1997 season might be the epitome of his toughness. Less than four months removed from tearing his ACL and MCL in the 49ers' first game of the season, Rice returned for a Monday night game against the Broncos in mid-December. He caught three passes in the game, including a 14-yard touchdown that put San Francisco on the board. However, he was hit on the play by Steve Atwater and fell onto his left knee, the same one that was hurt in the opener. What was first believed to be a bruise turned out to be a broken kneecap. The 14 regular-season games Rice missed that season were the only ones he ever missed due to injury in his career.

2. Dwight Clark is known for "The Catch," a six-yard touchdown in the final minute of the NFC Championship game in January 1982 that propelled the 49ers to their first Super Bowl appearance. According to legend, Clark was only discovered by the 49ers after serving as one of the receivers in San Francisco's workout with Clemson quarterback Steve Fuller. As the story is told, Clark was headed out to play golf when he got a call asking him to be a receiver for Fuller. Despite Clark having only 33 catches and four touchdowns in 34 games at Clemson, Bill Walsh drafted him in the 10th round of the 1979 NFL Draft. Clark

went on to catch 506 passes for 6,750 yards and 48 touchdowns in nine seasons with the 49ers.

3. The 49ers have only had five passes of more than 90 yards in the franchise's history, and John Taylor was on the receiving end of three of them. He is the only player in NFL history to have two 90-plus-yard touchdown catches in the same game, a feat he accomplished in a memorable Monday night performance in 1989. He caught 11 passes for 286 yards against the Los Angeles Rams on December 11, 1989, to help the 49ers overcome an early 17-0 deficit to win the game and clinch homefield advantage in the playoffs. It was the only time Taylor ever had a 200-yard receiving game, which stood for six years as the franchise record for most receiving yards in a game.

4. Gene Washington was the first black quarterback at Stanford before switching to wide receiver and becoming an All-American at the position. His name is still all over the 49ers' record book as he ranks 4th in receiving yards (6,664), 3rd in receiving touchdowns (59) and holds the record for career receiving average at 18 yards per reception. After retiring as a player, Washington eventually became the NFL's director of football operations from 1994-2009, handling the league's discipline for players.

5. Before the alley-oop became synonymous with basketball dunks, it was associated with 49ers receiver R.C. Owens. The term originated from Owens's jumping ability where he would leap over defenders for lofted passes from

quarterback Y.A. Tittle. It first debuted in a 1957 game and became Owens's nickname during his five-year career with the team. While playing for the Baltimore Colts in 1962, Owens blocked an extra point by simply leaping near the goal post—a play that was banned the following season by the NFL. He was also a basketball player at the College of Idaho and notched a double-double in every game he played. He was teammates at the school with Elgin Baylor and was drafted by the NBA's Minneapolis Lakers as well as the 49ers.

6. Terrell Owens was known for his antics as much as his talent during his Hall of Fame career. His first famous moment came in 2000 when he scored a touchdown in Dallas, then ran to midfield and celebrated on the Cowboys' star. However, he is probably still best remembered for a Monday night in 2002 in Seattle. Owens caught the game-winning touchdown over Seahawks cornerback Shawn Springs and pulled out a Sharpie from his sock and autographed the football. The ball was given to Greg Eastman, who was the financial advisor for both Owens and Springs at the time.

7. Brent Jones wasn't supposed to be part of the 49ers organization in 1987. Pittsburgh drafted him in the 5th round of the 1986 NFL Draft and planned for him to be their tight end of the future. However, he was in a car accident five days after being drafted and herniated a disc in his neck. He was out for a few months, but the Steelers were patient with him as he recovered. A month into the

1986 season, that patience wore out, and Jones was part of a bunch of cuts in order to save costs. The 49ers invited him to training camp in 1987, and Jones ended up playing 164 games for the franchise over the next 11 seasons.

8. Ten years after drafting Jerry Rice in the 1st round, the 49ers took another wideout with the 10th overall pick of the 1995 NFL Draft. J.J. Stokes was the first of five wide receivers San Francisco has picked in the 1st round over the last 35 years, all of whom have combined for only 44% of Rice's total yards with the team. The 49ers struck out on 2004 pick Rashaun Woods and 2012 selection A.J. Jenkins, but 2009 1st rounder Michael Crabtree had 347 receptions for 4,327 yards and 26 touchdowns in six seasons with the team. The fifth 1st round wide receiver is 2020 draft pick Brandon Aiyuk out of Arizona State, who was drafted 25th overall.

9. Vernon Davis has 10 credits on his IMDB page as an actor, and he's played himself three times. He appeared as himself in a 2013 episode of *The League*, a television show about a group of fantasy-football obsessed friends. In 2016, he guest starred on an episode of comedian Amy Schumer's sketch comedy show, *Inside Amy Schumer*. Davis also played himself in the 2017 blockbuster *Baywatch*, which starred Zac Efron, Dwayne "The Rock" Johnson, and Priyanka Chopra.

10. George Kittle was far and away the 49ers' best receiving threat in his record-breaking 2018 season. His 88

receptions were more than double the second-leading receiver, and he had nearly 1,000 more yards than his closest teammate. His 870 yards after The Catch led the league and was the most for any receiver since 2010, until it was broken in 2019 by Christian McCaffrey. Kittle has the second-most receiving yards for a tight end over the last three years, with 2,945 yards, but he has only caught 12 touchdowns in that span.

CHAPTER 7:

TRENCH WARFARE

QUIZ TIME!

1. Which pass rusher holds the record for the most sacks in their 49ers career?

    a. Bryant Young

    b. Aldon Smith

    c. Charles Haley

    d. Ahmad Brooks

2. Which anchor of the San Francisco offensive line holds the record for most consecutive games played at 208?

    a. Joe Staley

    b. Bob St. Clair

    c. Len Rohde

    d. Leo Nomellini

3. As of the end of the 2019 season, how many front seven players have been inducted into the 49ers Hall of Fame?

    a. 3

    b. 4

c. 5

d. 6

4. Bob St. Clair is one of the five 49ers players to have his number retired in the 1970s.

    a. True

    b. False

5. How many field goals did Bob St. Clair block in 1956?

    a. 10

    b. 8

    c. 6

    d. 4

6. Before Aldon Smith broke it in 2012, who held the 49ers' record for most sacks in a season?

    a. Charles Haley

    b. Leo Nomellini

    c. Tim Harris

    d. Fred Dean

7. Which of these pass rushers did NOT have at least 10 sacks as a rookie?

    a. Aldon Smith

    b. Nick Bosa

    c. Dana Stubblefield

    d. Charles Haley

8. Leo Nomellini was an All-NFL player on both the offensive and defensive lines during his career.

a. True

b. False

9. Which Hall-of-Famer, who spent three seasons or less with the 49ers, did NOT have 10 career sacks with San Francisco?

a. Chris Doleman

b. Kevin Greene

c. Richard Dent

d. Rickey Jackson

10. Before drafting a wide receiver in the 1st round in 2020, how many consecutive years did San Francisco select a lineman with its first pick in the draft?

a. 2

b. 3

c. 4

d. 5

11. The three linemen who have had their numbers retired for the franchise all suited up for the franchise in the same season.

a. True

b. False

12. Which of these offensive linemen did NOT start three Super Bowls for the 49ers?

a. Randy Cross

b. Bubba Paris

c. Jesse Sapolu

d. Harris Barton

13. At which position did four-time Pro Bowler Bruce Bosley NEVER start for San Francisco?

   a. Offensive guard
   b. Center
   c. Defensive end
   d. Offensive tackle

14. Who was the first player to return a fumble for a touchdown in 49ers history?

   a. Charlie Krueger
   b. Leo Nomellini
   c. Matt Hazeltine
   d. Abe Woodson

15. Who was the 21-year offensive line coach who was part of all five 49ers Super Bowl victories?

   a. Dick Stanfel
   b. Bobb McKittrick
   c. Ernie Zwahlen
   d. Bob St. Clair

16. Who holds the 49ers' record for most sacks in a playoff game?

   a. Ahmad Brooks
   b. Pierce Holt
   c. DeForest Buckner
   d. Arik Armstead

17. Which offensive lineman ranks second to Jerry Rice for most playoff games played with San Francisco?

a. Harris Barton

b. Joe Staley

c. Jesse Sapolu

d. Randy Cross

18. Who was the last San Francisco defensive lineman to return an interception for a touchdown?

a. Justin Smith

b. DeForest Buckner

c. Solomon Thomas

d. Ray McDonald

19. Mike Iupati is the last 49ers offensive lineman to be named a First Team All-Pro.

a. True

b. False

20. Which of these Joe Staley stats is NOT true?

a. 5-time Pro Bowler

b. 3 career receptions

c. 18 career tackles

d. 7 career fumble recoveries

QUIZ ANSWERS

1. A – Bryant Young

2. C – Len Rohde

3. C – 5

4. B – False

5. A – 10

6. D – Fred Dean

7. B – Nick Bosa

8. A – True

9. C – Richard Dent

10. D – 5

11. A – True

12. B – Bubba Paris

13. D – Offensive tackle

14. C – Matt Hazeltine

15. B – Bobb McKittrick

16. B – Pierce Holt

17. C – Jesse Sapolu

18. D – Ray McDonald

19. A – True

20. A – 5-time Pro Bowler

DID YOU KNOW?

1. Joe Staley was the first rookie offensive lineman to start every game of a season in 39 years and played every single snap at right tackle in 2007. He repeated the feat in 2008 and started all 16 games in eight total seasons with the franchise. His 190 appearances for the 49ers are the 9th most all-time and 3rd among offensive linemen. He was one of two players who played on both of the 49ers Super Bowl teams in the twenty-first century.

2. Bob St. Clair was nicknamed "The Geek" by his teammates for his peculiar eating habits. St. Clair ate most of his meat raw, which reminded Bruno Banducci of a character called "The Geek," who was kept in a cage and fed live animals. St. Clair claims he acquired his taste for raw meat from his grandmother, who was Yaqui Indian and fed him blood gravy with bits of raw beef.

3. Leo Nomellini was the last player from San Francisco's first NFL roster in 1950 to leave the team when he retired after the 1963 season. Born in Italy, Nomellini moved to Chicago as a young child and started working in high school to support his family. He never saw a football game before playing in one as a member of the Marines in Cherry Point, North Carolina. He never saw a college football game before becoming a four-year starter at the University of Minnesota.

4. After retiring from the NFL, Charlie Krueger sued the 49ers for fraud, claiming the organization lied to him about the severity of his knee injuries. He won his case unanimously in 1987 when the First District Court of Appeal in California agreed that the 49ers did not properly warn Krueger of the risks he was in while injecting him with painkillers for most of his final 10 seasons in the league. In the court's opinion, written by Justice William Newsom, it says Krueger suffered from traumatic arthritis and had begun an irreversible, degenerative process in his knee. As a result, he could no longer stand for prolonged periods, could not run, and suffers while walking up and down stairs. The Superior Court later awarded Krueger $2.36 million in damages.

5. San Francisco coach Bill Walsh was so upset with offensive tackle Bubba Paris's weight control issues that Walsh sent Paris to a weight-loss clinic. Paris arrived to training camp in 1988 at 335 pounds, which proved to be the final straw for Walsh. Paris was the 49ers' starting left tackle from 1983-86, but lost his job in the middle of the 1987 season only to regain it when his replacement, Steve Wallace, was injured. Wallace eventually kept the spot in 1988, but Paris started the entire 1989 and 1990 seasons before playing in Indianapolis in 1991.

6. Jeremy Newberry was a do-it-all offensive lineman for the 49ers in his first three seasons in the league. He missed his rookie year in 1998 with a knee injury, but he started at both right guard and right tackle in 1999. He moved back to his

preferred position at center for the 2000 season and was named to the Pro Bowl in 2001 and 2002. Eventually knee problems got the better of him and a 2005 microfracture surgery did not solve the woes. He eventually retired in 2009 just months after signing with the Atlanta Falcons.

7. Mike Iupati has made a tour of the NFC West after being selected in the 1st round in 2010 by the 49ers. He played five seasons in San Francisco and was named to three Pro Bowls and was a 2012 First Team All-Pro selection. When his rookie deal ended in San Francisco, he signed a contract with the Arizona Cardinals, then moved on to Seattle in 2019 after four years with the Cardinals. Iupati was one of three San Francisco 1st round draft picks who started on the 2012 team that returned the 49ers to the Super Bowl.

8. Few trades changed the course of 49ers history more than their 1981 acquisition of Fred Dean from the San Diego Chargers. Dean had 12 sacks in 11 games for the 49ers and helped San Francisco win its first Super Bowl later that season. Two years later, Dean was even better with 17.5 sacks in 16 games played, including a team-record 6 sacks in one game against New Orleans on November 13. That tally stood as the NFL record for seven years, but Dean became a situational pass rusher when the 49ers won the Super Bowl in 1984, then retired in 1985 after registering just three sacks in 16 games.

9. Aldon Smith is the classic case of what could have been for the 49ers. The pass rusher was the fastest in league history

to reach 30 sacks, doing so in just 27 games with San Francisco. He set the 49ers record in his second year in the league, with 19.5 sacks, and ranks 6th on the franchise's all-time sacks list with 44 in 50 games over four seasons with the team. What held back Smith from his potential was his alcohol abuse. He was arrested three times on suspicions of drunk driving in his first five years in the league, and was cut by the 49ers during training camp in 2015. Smith entered rehab in 2013, forcing him to miss five games, then was suspended for the first nine games of the 2014 season for violating the league's substance abuse and personal conduct policy. Smith was granted reinstatement into the league in May 2020 after being indefinitely suspended by the league in 2015 for his substance abuse issues.

10. The 49ers had a terrifying duo of Oregon products on its defensive line in 2018 and 2019, with Arik Armstead and DeForest Buckner. Armstead had a career-high 10 sacks in 2019, coming close to matching the 12 Buckner produced in 2018. Buckner had just 7.5 sacks in 2019, but recovered four fumbles and finished fourth on the team with 62 tackles. The pair were the 49ers' 1st round picks in consecutive seasons and were a critical part in San Francisco's defense as the 49ers dominated the NFC en route to the Super Bowl.

CHAPTER 8:

NO AIR ZONE

QUIZ TIME!

1. Before Richard Sherman was named to the Pro Bowl after the 2019 season, who was the last 49ers defensive back to be invited to the Pro Bowl?

   a. Eric Reid
   b. Carlos Rogers
   c. Dashon Goldson
   d. Antoine Bethea

2. When did Deion Sanders play his one season with the 49ers?

   a. 1993
   b. 1994
   c. 1995
   d. 1996

3. The 10 longest interception returns in 49ers history all went for touchdowns.

a. True

b. False

4. Who is the only 49ers player to ever return two interceptions for touchdowns in the same game?

a. Ken Norton

b. Ronnie Lott

c. Deion Sanders

d. Jimmy Johnson

5. How many defensive backs have played 100 games for the 49ers?

a. 8

b. 9

c. 10

d. 11

6. Which linebacker does not share the San Francisco record for most interceptions by a non-defensive back in a season?

a. Jim Fahnhorst

b. Frank Nunley

c. Dave Wilcox

d. Keena Turner

7. Who was the first San Francisco secondary member to be named an All-Pro by the Associated Press?

a. Jimmy Johnson

b. Lowell Wagner

c. Rex Berry

d. Jim Cason

8. Who has the most interceptions in 49ers history without ever returning one for a touchdown?

    a. Dave Baker
    b. Kermit Alexander
    c. Jimmy Johnson
    d. Lowell Wagner

9. Tony Dungy was elected to the Pro Football Hall of Fame as a coach, but he played three seasons in the NFL prior to joining the coaching ranks. How many games did Dungy start for the 49ers in his career?

    a. 3
    b. 5
    c. 7
    d. 9

10. The 1951 49ers hold the team record for most interceptions per game, with 33 in just 12 games. How many different players recorded an interception that season?

    a. 9
    b. 8
    c. 7
    d. 6

11. How many different players had an interception in the 1986 season opener when the 49ers set the team record for most interceptions in a game?

    a. 5
    b. 6

c. 7

d. 8

12. Ronnie Lott was named the Defensive Rookie of the Year in 1981.

   a. True

   b. False

13. Ronnie Lott holds the 49ers' record for most interception return yards in a career. How many yards does he have?

   a. 587

   b. 609

   c. 643

   d. 691

14. How many games did Ronnie Lott play when he led the league with 10 interceptions in 1986?

   a. 13

   b. 14

   c. 15

   d. 16

15. Which defensive back was traded to the Pittsburgh Steelers in 1960 in exchange for the 1st round pick that San Francisco used to draft Jimmy Johnson?

   a. Dick Moegle

   b. Abe Woodson

   c. Dave Baker

   d. Lowell Wagner

16. How many passes did Hall-of-Famer Jimmy Johnson intercept as a rookie?

    a. 3
    b. 4
    c. 5
    d. 6

17. Jimmy Johnson had at least one interception in every year of his career that he played defense.

    a. True
    b. False

18. Which defensive back holds the 49ers' record for career kickoff return touchdowns and is the only one who has multiple kickoff return touchdowns in a season?

    a. Allen Rossum
    b. Dana McLemore
    c. Joe Arenas
    d. Abe Woodson

19. Who has the most interceptions for the 49ers in the twenty-first century?

    a. Dashon Goldson
    b. Eric Reid
    c. Walt Harris
    d. Tony Parrish

20. San Francisco only had two interceptions during the 2018 season, a franchise low. Which two players intercepted those passes?

a. Fred Warner and Jimmie Ward
b. Richard Sherman and Ahkello Witherspoon
c. Antone Exum Jr. and Jaquiski Tartt
d. K'Waun Williams and Richard Sherman

QUIZ ANSWERS

1. D – Antoine Bethea

2. B – 1994

3. B – False

4. A – Ken Norton

5. B – 9

6. C – Dave Wilcox

7. D – Jim Cason

8. D – Lowell Wagner

9. C – 7

10. A – 9

11. B – 6

12. B – False

13. C – 643

14. B – 14

15. A – Dick Moegle

16. C – 5

17. A – True

18. D – Abe Woodson

19. D – Tony Parrish

20. C – Antone Exum Jr. and Jaquiski Tartt

DID YOU KNOW?

1. Ronnie Lott was once described as "a middle linebacker playing safety" by Hall of Fame coach Tom Landry, who added, Lott "may dominate the secondary better than anyone I've seen." Lott was a dynamo at the back of the 49ers defense for 148 total games in 10 seasons, from 1981 to 1990. San Francisco won its division eight times while Lott was patrolling the secondary, and was named an All-Pro eight times in his Hall of Fame career. He still holds the 49ers' record for most career interceptions (51), single-season interceptions (10), and pick-sixes (5) in addition to a franchise-best eight interceptions in the playoffs.

2. Jimmy Johnson might not even be the best athlete in his own family. His brother, Rafer Johnson, won the silver medal in the men's decathlon at the 1956 Summer Olympics, then followed up four years later by winning the gold medal in Rome. He was the American flag-bearer at the opening ceremonies for the 1960 Summer Olympics, then was given the ultimate honor of lighting the Olympic torch to start the 1984 Summer Olympics in Los Angeles. Rafer Johnson was also famous for being part of the group that tackled Sirhan Sirhan in 1968 after he fatally wounded U.S. Senator and presidential hopeful Robert F. Kennedy.

3. Deion Sanders only spent one season in San Francisco, but what a year it was for the Hall-of-Famer. Sanders had six

interceptions and returned them for a team-record 303 yards, and three of those returns went for touchdowns, also a team record. He added two more interceptions in the playoffs as the 49ers won the Super Bowl, giving him the first of his two Super Bowl rings. The performance earned him Associated Press NFL Defensive Player of the Year honors for the only time in his career.

4. Perhaps a little before his time, Rex Berry was the type of ball-hawking safety who would have plenty of success in the modern game. Instead, Berry dominated the secondary in the 1950s with 22 interceptions over six seasons for the 49ers. He returned three of those interceptions for touchdowns, which stood as the team record until Ronnie Lott came to town. Berry retired in 1957, leaving his yearly salary of $12,500 to become a chemical salesman for U.S. Steel.

5. Abe Woodson was a defensive back who made his name returning kickoffs for the 49ers from 1958 until 1964. In addition to holding the 49ers' record for career kick return average, he ranks 5th all-time in NFL history in kick return average. He does not hold the record for best average kick return in a season, but he holds five of the top 10 slots in team history and also led the NFL in average three times, which is tied for the most in league history. Woodson also holds the record for most kickoff return touchdowns, with five, and the longest kick return at 105 yards, set on November 8, 1959, against the Rams.

6. A broken leg and ankle in 2005 derailed what was a promising future for Tony Parrish in San Francisco. After signing as a free agent in 2002, Parrish came into his own as a ball-hawking safety in the 49ers secondary. He had seven interceptions in his first season, then had an NFL-best nine in 2003 when he was named a Second Team All-Pro. He had four interceptions in 2004, then had two more in nine games in 2005 before breaking his leg. He retired from the NFL in 2006, then tried to make a comeback with the Las Vegas Locomotives of the United Football League in 2009, helping the franchise win the championship that season. His 22 interceptions in 66 games for San Francisco still ranks 7th in team history.

7. Tim McKyer burst onto the scene as a rookie for San Francisco in 1986 with six interceptions, one shy of the record Ronnie Lott set five years earlier. He picked off seven passes in his third season in the league and had 16 in four seasons with the 49ers. His connection to the 49ers didn't end there, however. As his career was winding down in 1995, McKyer was playing for the expansion Carolina Panthers in San Francisco when he intercepted Elvis Grbac and returned it 96 yards for a touchdown in a 13-7 Panthers win.

8. Eric Reid was a productive member of the 49ers secondary from 2013-17, but his impact on the game also extended beyond the field. Reid was the first to join then-teammate Colin Kaepernick in kneeling during the national anthem as a protest to racial injustice, and remained outspoken

even after Kaepernick was not re-signed about the way the league was treating his friend. When Reid's contract expired after the 2017 season, San Francisco elected not to renew the deal until into the 2018 season when the Carolina Panthers eventually signed him. Reid had 10 interceptions and made 318 tackles in 70 games with the 49ers.

9. Before they were teammates in the NFL, Jimmie Ward and Dontae Johnson built a strong relationship with one another at the 2014 Senior Bowl in Mobile, Alabama. The two were roommates at the week-long all-star game for college players while teammates on the North team for the game. Ward was San Francisco's 1st round draft pick in 2014 and was one of the first to reach out to Johnson when the 49ers used its second 4th round pick on him that same season. After playing for three teams in an injury-plagued 2018 season, Johnson returned to the 49ers in 2019.

10. Richard Sherman has endeared himself to 49ers fans with his play in 2018 and 2019, but he wasn't always well-liked in San Francisco. Sherman was at the center of controversy in the NFC Championship game in the 2013-14 season after batting away a Colin Kaepernick pass to Michael Crabtree into the arms of a teammate for a game-sealing interception to send the Seahawks to the Super Bowl. After the game, an animated Sherman told Fox's Erin Andrews, "I'm the best cornerback in the game. When you try me with a sorry receiver like Crabtree, that's the result you are going to get. Don't you ever talk about me."

CHAPTER 9:

SUPER BOWL SALUTE

QUIZ TIME!

1. How many times have the 49ers played in the Super Bowl?

   a. 6

   b. 7

   c. 8

   d. 9.

2. Which team was the only one to play the 49ers twice in the Super Bowl?

   a. San Diego Chargers

   b. Denver Broncos

   c. Cincinnati Bengals

   d. Miami Dolphins

3. Who was the only non-quarterback to win Super Bowl MVP in San Francisco's five victories?

   a. Jerry Rice

   b. John Taylor

   c. Ronnie Lott

   d. Roger Craig

4. How long was the longest field goal the 49ers have made in a Super Bowl?

   a. 39 yards
   b. 40 yards
   c. 41 yards
   d. 42 yards

5. Who has scored the most career rushing touchdowns in Super Bowls for the 49ers?

   a. Roger Craig
   b. Ricky Watters
   c. Joe Montana
   d. Tom Rathman

6. When the Baltimore Ravens beat the 49ers in Super Bowl XLVII, they overtook San Francisco as the only team to win multiple Super Bowls without losing one.

   a. True
   b. False

7. The 49ers hold the record for largest margin of victory in the Super Bowl with 55-10 in which Super Bowl?

   a. XXIII
   b. XXIV
   c. XIX
   d. XXIX

8. Which team did the 49ers beat in the only Super Bowl held at Stanford Stadium?

a. San Diego Chargers

b. Denver Broncos

c. Miami Dolphins

d. Oakland Raiders

9. Three of the five players who share the record for most touchdowns in a Super Bowl played for the 49ers when they set the record. Which player is NOT part of that tie?

a. Ricky Watters

b. Roger Craig

c. Jerry Rice

d. Dwight Clark

10. If you add up the numbers of every Super Bowl the 49ers appeared in, what would the total be?

a. 197

b. 209

c. 212

d. 228

11. Who scored the 49ers' first touchdown in a Super Bowl?

a. Joe Montana

b. Roger Craig

c. Dwight Clark

d. Earl Cooper

12. How many rushing yards did San Francisco produce in its win in Super Bowl XIX?

a. 163

b. 182

c. 198

d. 211

13. No 49ers wide receiver caught a touchdown in the Super Bowl until the fourth quarter of Super Bowl XXIII.

    a. True

    b. False

14. Joe Montana set the 49ers' record for most passing yards in a playoff game in San Francisco's Super Bowl XXIII victory. How many yards did Montana throw for in the only Super Bowl in which he was not named MVP?

    a. 333

    b. 342

    c. 357

    d. 366

15. Who was the only player besides Jerry Rice to score multiple touchdowns in San Francisco's rout in Super Bowl XXIV?

    a. Brent Jones

    b. John Taylor

    c. Roger Craig

    d. Tom Rathman

16. How many plays did it take for the 49ers to score a touchdown in Super Bowl XXIX?

    a. 5

    b. 4

    c. 3

    d. 2

17. The 49ers held a lead in Super Bowl XLVII.

    a. True
    b. False

18. Colin Kaepernick set a record for longest touchdown run by a quarterback in Super Bowl history in Super Bowl XLVII. How long was his scoring run?

    a. 11 yards
    b. 13 yards
    c. 15 yards
    d. 17 yards

19. Which receiver set a Super Bowl record with a 32-yard run and 53 rushing yards against the Kansas City Chiefs?

    a. Deebo Samuels
    b. George Kittle
    c. Emmanuel Sanders
    d. Marquise Goodwin

20. How many times did San Francisco sack Patrick Mahomes in its Super Bowl loss to the Chiefs?

    a. 1
    b. 2
    c. 3
    d. 4

QUIZ ANSWERS

1. B – 7

2. C – Cincinnati Bengals

3. A – Jerry Rice

4. D – 42 yards

5. D – Tom Rathman

6. A – True

7. B – XXIV

8. C – Miami Dolphins

9. D – Dwight Clark

10. C – 212

11. A – Joe Montana

12. D – 211

13. A – True

14. C – 357

15. D – Tom Rathman

16. C – 3

17. B – False

18. C – 15 yards

19. A – Deebo Samuels

20. D – 4

DID YOU KNOW?

1. Ray Wersching booted home four field goals in San Francisco's first Super Bowl win—Super Bowl XVI against Cincinnati—and is one of two kickers to ever make four field goals in a Super Bowl. Those four in a game are still the 49ers' team record for most field goals in a playoff game, as are the 13 total field goals he hit in the postseason in his career. His five career field goals in Super Bowls ranks 3rd all-time, but he made all five of his career attempts, too, something the two kickers ahead of him did not accomplish. Only one of Wersching's field goals was longer than 30 yards, but the 40-yarder he hit in the fourth quarter of Super Bowl XVI helped put the game out of reach.

2. Joe Montana's three Super Bowl MVPs are impressive as are many of the gaudy statistics he put up in the Super Bowl. But the most impressive is still the fact Montana did not throw a single interception in 122 pass attempts across four Super Bowl appearances. His 147.6 passer rating in Super Bowl XXIV is still the best single-game total in 49ers postseason history, and his 127.8 rating in Super Bowls is the best in NFL history. He ran for two rushing touchdowns, including a one-yard sneak in the first quarter of Super Bowl XVI, which was San Francisco's first touchdown in a Super Bowl. He was a deserving three-time Super Bowl MVP, and still delivered the play of the

game in the one Super Bowl in which he wasn't named MVP.

3. When it comes to receiving records in the Super Bowl, there are few that don't belong to Hall-of-Famer Jerry Rice. He has the most receptions in a career (33), most career yards (589), and most yards in a game (215 in winning Super Bowl MVP in Super Bowl XIII). Rice's eight career receiving touchdowns are far and away the most in a Super Bowl, but 2nd place is a five-way tie with three. Meanwhile, Rice matched that total in a single Super Bowl twice in his career, which is also a record he owns. Those eight touchdowns also lead all players—rushing and receiving—and his 48 points from those scores are also tops in league history.

4. Tom Rathman was quietly such a pivotal part of the 1988 and 1989 Super Bowl championship teams for the 49ers with a franchise-record three Super Bowl rushing touchdowns in his career. Rathman is still the only San Francisco 49ers running back to rush for two touchdowns in the Super Bowl, accomplishing the feat against Denver in Super Bowl XXIV. It was his 16-yard reception that set up the opening field goal of Super Bowl XXIII against the Bengals. He accounted for five first downs, including two fourth-down conversions, in addition to his two touchdowns in Super Bowl XXIV. In his two Super Bowl appearances, he had 16 carries for 61 yards and added five catches for 59 yards as well.

5. The most iconic drive in San Francisco 49ers history began with a mistake. A penalty set up the 49ers at their own 8-yard line instead of the 20 with just 3:20 left in Super Bowl XXIII. Joe Montana connected on five straight passes mixed in with two Roger Craig runs to set up the ball at the Cincinnati 35-yard line. A holding penalty pushed back San Francisco 10 yards, but Montana connected with Jerry Rice for 27 yards to recoup the lost yardage. A short pass to Craig and subsequent timeout left San Francisco with a second down from the Bengals' 10. The rest is history, of course, as Montana found John Taylor in the middle of the end zone for the winning touchdown, lifting the 49ers to their second Super Bowl title.

6. San Francisco became the fifth team—and fourth franchise—to win consecutive Super Bowls when it won Super Bowls XXIII and XXIV after the 1988 and 1989 seasons. The games could not have been any different for the 49ers, either. San Francisco needed the aforementioned last-minute heroics of Joe Montana and John Taylor to escape Cincinnati in Super Bowl XXIII in Miami. The following year, the 49ers took no prisoners at the Superdome with 41 points in the first 35 minutes of the game for an eventual 55-10 walloping of the Denver Broncos. San Francisco intercepted John Elway twice and sacked the Broncos quarterback four times while limiting him to just 108 passing yards.

7. The 49ers' fifth Super Bowl victory rivaled their fourth in many ways as the records they set in trouncing the

Broncos were in jeopardy against the Chargers. Steve Young broke Joe Montana's record with six touchdown tosses, and Jerry Rice tied his own record with three touchdown catches in a 49-26 win over San Diego in Miami. That game is still the highest-scoring Super Bowl in league history and has the record for most combined touchdowns as well, with 75 points and 10 touchdowns.

8. In 2011, Jim and John Harbaugh became the first brothers to coach against each other in an NFL game. The following season, they upped the stakes as the first brothers to lead their teams to the Super Bowl against one another. John, the big brother by a little more than a year, and the Ravens won both contests over Jim and the 49ers. After the game, John Harbaugh told the media about feeling for his brother, "It's tough. It's very tough. It's a lot tougher than I thought it was going to be. It's very painful."

9. Super Bowl XLVII is probably most remembered for the blackout at the Superdome that delayed the game 34 minutes. It might have been the best thing that could have happened for the 49ers, who were trailing 28-6 early in the third quarter when the lights went out. San Francisco scored 17 straight points after the game resumed to cut the deficit to just five points, then held the Ravens to field goal on their first drive of the fourth quarter. Colin Kaepernick ran for his 15-yard score on the next drive, bringing the 49ers within a two-point conversion of a tie, but the pass for Randy Moss fell incomplete. That was the closest San Francisco would come to completing its rally, as the 49ers

felt the pain of losing a Super Bowl for the first time in franchise history.

10. The final nine minutes of Super Bowl LIV were tough for the 49ers. San Francisco entered the fourth quarter with a 20-10 lead, then intercepted Patrick Mahomes in the red zone on the first drive of the fourth. After the 49ers had to punt following the interception, they pinned the Chiefs to a third-and-15, but Mahomes found Tyreek Hill for 44 yards to jump-start the rally. Kansas City would score on that drive and its next two to cement the 31-20 win. The 21 points San Francisco allowed in the fourth quarter matched the Buffalo Bills from Super Bowl XXVII as the most points allowed in the final 15 minutes of a Super Bowl.

CHAPTER 10:

SHINING THE BUSTS

QUIZ TIME!

1. In which year were the first two San Francisco 49ers inducted into the Pro Football Hall of Fame?

    a. 1965

    b. 1967

    c. 1969

    d. 1971.

2. How many people enshrined in the Pro Football Hall of Fame as players played at least one season for the 49ers?

    a. 22

    b. 24

    c. 26

    d. 28

3. In which decade have the most 49ers been inducted into the Hall of Fame?

    a. 1980s

    b. 1990s

c. 2000s

d. 2010s

4. Y.A. Tittle never threw more interceptions than touchdowns in his 10 seasons with the 49ers.

a. True

b. False

5. One of the NFL's original ironmen, Leo Nomellini never missed a game during his 14-year career in San Francisco. How many consecutive games did Nomellini play for the 49ers?

a. 170

b. 174

c. 179

d. 186

6. How tall was Bob St. Clair during his playing days?

a. 6 feet 6 inches

b. 6 feet 7 inches

c. 6 feet 8 inches

d. 6 feet 9 inches

7. How many touchdowns did Joe Perry run for as a member of the San Francisco 49ers?

a. 60

b. 64

c. 68

d. 72

8. How many times was Dave Wilcox selected for the Pro Bowl?

    a. 4
    b. 5
    c. 6
    d. 7

9. Ed DeBartolo Jr. is the most recent member from the 49ers dynasty of the 1980s to be inducted into the Hall of Fame.

    a. True
    b. False

10. Who was the quarterback who felt Fred Dean's wrath in 1983 when he set the franchise record with six sacks in a game?

    a. Dave Wilson
    b. Archie Manning
    c. Ken Stabler
    d. Richard Todd

11. Who was the last of San Francisco's famed Million Dollar Backfield to earn election into the Hall of Fame?

    a. Hugh McElhenny
    b. John Henry Johnson
    c. Joe Perry
    d. Y.A. Tittle

12. How old was Bill Walsh when he was named the 49ers' head coach in 1979?

a. 38

b. 42

c. 45

d. 47

13. Ronnie Lott led the 49ers in interceptions five times in 10 seasons with the team. How many consecutive years did Lott lead the team in picks?

a. 2

b. 3

c. 4

d. 5

14. How many times did Charles Haley hit double digits in sacks during his original six-year tenure in San Francisco?

a. 3

b. 4

c. 5

d. 6

15. On December 17, 2000, Terrell Owens set the 49ers' record for most receptions in a game when he hauled in how many passes against Chicago?

a. 17

b. 28

c. 19

d. 20

16. Jimmy Johnson played offense during his second year in the league, and ranked 2nd on the 49ers in receptions,

receiving yards, and touchdowns. How many passes did he catch that season?

a. 28
b. 31
c. 34
d. 39

17. Steve Young ranks in the top 10 in 49ers history for rushing yards.

a. True
b. False

18. In which Super Bowl winning season did Joe Montana complete less than 60% of his passes for the only time in his career as the 49ers' starter?

a. 1984
b. 1981
c. 1989
d. 1988

19. How many times did Jerry Rice catch at least 100 passes for the 49ers?

a. 2
b. 3
c. 4
d. 5

20. How many of the 49ers' Hall-of-Famers have their jersey number retired by the franchise?

a. 9
b. 10
c. 11
d. 12

QUIZ ANSWERS

1. C – 1969

2. C – 26

3. D – 2010s

4. B – False

5. B – 174

6. D – 6 feet 9 inches

7. C – 68

8. D – 7

9. A – True

10. A – Dave Wilson

11. B – John Henry Johnson

12. D – 47

13. C – 4

14. B – 4

15. D – 20

16. C – 34

17. A – True

18. D – 1988

19. C – 4

20. A – 9

DID YOU KNOW?

1. July 29, 2000, was San Francisco 49ers Day in Canton, Ohio. The Pro Football Hall of Fame welcomed five new members that day, and three of them had significant ties to the 49ers. Joe Montana, Ronnie Lott, and Dave Wilcox all were inducted that day into the Hall of Fame, bridging two eras of 49ers history. The only other time two 49ers have been inducted into the Hall of Fame at the same time was 1969 when Leo Nomellini and Joe Perry were both voted into the Hall. Those two were the first two members of the franchise to be enshrined in Canton.

2. Jimmy Johnson had a topsy-turvy first three seasons with the 49ers as he kept changing sides of the ball, but he kept producing. He made five interceptions as a rookie defensive back in 1961, but the coaches still made him a receiver in 1962. He caught an 80-yard touchdown against the Bears and put up 181 yards against the Lions that year before switching back to defense. He finished with 47 interceptions and seven fumble recoveries for the 49ers and was an All-Pro from 1969-72 in the secondary.

3. Bill Walsh bookended his run as 49ers coach with stints as the head coach at nearby Stanford University. The Genius was 17-7 in his first two years as the Cardinals' coach before being lured away by the 49ers to build their dynasty. He returned to Palo Alto in 1992 and went 10-3

before he had two losing seasons in 1993 and 1994. Between his run in the college game, Walsh coached the most dominant team in the NFL, winning three Super Bowls and six division titles in 10 seasons. Remarkably, Walsh was only named the NFL Coach of the Year once—in 1981, when the 49ers went from 6-10 to 13-3 and their first Super Bowl title.

4. Ronnie Lott was a prolific defensive back, no matter where the 49ers elected to play him in the secondary. He was an All-Pro selection at three positions—cornerback, free safety, and strong safety—but he is still known largely for his work as a free safety for San Francisco. He racked up at least 100 tackles five times—just twice with the 49ers, though—and he led the league in interceptions twice. As a rookie in 1981, Lott had seven interceptions, and returned three of them for touchdowns, a total that would be tied for the 49ers career lead by itself. He had six seasons with at least five interceptions for the 49ers, including his record 10 in 14 games in 1988.

5. Dave Wilcox was known as "The Intimidator" for his aggressive style of play on the field, but he only missed one game in his career due to injury. In 11 seasons with the 49ers, Wilcox made 14 interceptions and recovered 12 fumbles, scoring once through both methods. His best season, though, came in 1973 when he compiled 104 tackles, including 13 for a loss, and forced four fumbles to go along with two interceptions. In their postseason analysis of every player's performance, the 49ers graded

most linebackers around a 750. In 1973, Wilcox's score was an impressive 1,306.

6. In his Hall of Fame induction speech, Ed DeBartolo Jr. told the story of the day the 49ers drafted Joe Montana. DeBartolo said he remembered being outside his office in Redwood City, California, when Bill Walsh asked him about taking a shot on a Notre Dame quarterback in the 3rd round of the 1979 NFL Draft. Being a Notre Dame alum himself, DeBartolo quipped, "How could you go wrong with somebody from Notre Dame." The day after selecting him, DeBartolo met Montana for the first time, and this is how the owner described his first impression: "I looked at him and almost fell over. He was a kid. He had a big Fu Manchu mustache. He looked like he weighed about 170 pounds. He was listed at 6'2", and he didn't look an inch past 6 foot. I said: Oh, dear God." It all seemed to work out just fine for DeBartolo, Montana, and the 49ers.

7. In his enshrinement speech, Jerry Rice made note that his first-ever flight was the one he took from Mississippi to San Francisco after being drafted. He called the flight "long" and "stomach-churning," and said, "I was scared to death, but excited at the same time. Scared about surviving the flight, excited like I am now because I knew I was joining a great team that had already won two Super Bowls." Rice went on to become the best receiver ever to play the game, being named a First Team All-Pro in 11 straight seasons while winning three Super Bowls with San Francisco.

8. Ed DeBartolo Jr. presented five different players for induction into the Hall of Fame on their enshrinement days before being inducted himself in 2016. Only Al Davis and Paul Brown introduced more men than DeBartolo Jr. The first time he did it was in 1993 when he introduced Bill Walsh on induction day. He also introduced Joe Montana in 2000, Fred Dean in 2008, Jerry Rice in 2010, and Charles Haley in 2015. But for his own induction, DeBartolo Jr. selected his daughter, Lisa Marie, but admitted it likely would have been Walsh had the coach still been alive for his induction. Walsh actually sent DeBartolo Jr. a congratulatory message posthumously, having prewritten a note and given it to his son, Greg, for this exact moment.

9. Seven different Hall-of-Famers played exactly one season for the 49ers, a total that includes Tony Dungy who was elected as a coach not a player. The 1994 Super Bowl winning team had two of those players—Richard Dent and Deion Sanders—and the 1997 squad had Kevin Greene and Rod Woodson. Bob Hayes played for San Francisco in 1975, and Randy Moss suited up for the 49ers in 2012 when they lost the Super Bowl to the Ravens.

10. sTerrell Owens declined to attend his enshrinement ceremony in Canton, Ohio, deciding instead to celebrate his induction at his alma mater, Tennessee-Chattanooga. He was never formally mentioned at any of the Hall of Fame events that weekend, though he was referenced when the collective 2018 Class was discussed. In his

speech in Chattanooga, Owens said he decided to forgo the festivities in Canton because of the voters, who he claimed "are not in alignment with the mission and core values of the Hall of Fame" for rejecting him the first two years he was on the ballot.

CHAPTER 11:

DRAFT DAY

QUIZ TIME!

1. Who was the first San Francisco draft pick of the NFL era?

   a. Billy Wilson

   b. Don Burke

   c. Leo Nomellini

   d. Y.A. Tittle

2. The San Francisco 49ers' first three 1st round draft picks as an NFL team all went on to be inducted into the Pro Football Hall of Fame.

   a. True

   b. False

3. How many Hall-of-Famers have the 49ers drafted in their history?

   a. 9

   b. 10

   c. 11

   d. 12

4. In 1953, the 49ers held the 1st overall pick for the first of three times in franchise history. Who did they select to open the draft?

   a. Dick Moegle
   b. Harry Babcock
   c. Bob St. Clair
   d. Tom Stolhandske

5. Which two-time All-Pro quarterback did the 49ers draft with the 2nd overall pick in 1956?

   a. Bart Starr
   b. Earl Morrall
   c. John Brodie
   d. Eagle Day

6. Although he ended up not signing with the team, which future Hall-of-Famer did the 49ers draft with their 1st pick in the 1962 NFL Draft?

   a. Mick Tingelhoff
   b. Bobby Mitchell
   c. Merlin Olsen
   d. Lance Alworth

7. The 49ers picked Heisman Trophy winner Steve Spurrier with the first of two 1st round picks in 1967, but eight picks later took which offensive lineman from Northwestern who started nine seasons at right tackle for the team?

   a. Tom Holzer
   b. Cas Banazsek

c. Woody Peoples

d. Forrest Blue

8. San Francisco might have traded its two 1st round picks in 1976 to acquire Jim Plunkett, but which two key members of the offensive line that paved the way to the 49ers first two Super Bowl titles did the 49ers draft that season?

   a. John Ayers and Keith Fahnhorst

   b. Randy Cross and John Ayers

   c. Bubba Paris and Fred Quillan

   d. Randy Cross and Fred Quillan

9. How many quarterbacks were chosen before San Francisco wisely swooped in and selected Joe Montana at 82nd overall in 1979?

   a. 5

   b. 4

   c. 3

   d. 2

10. In which round of the 1983 NFL Draft did the 49ers scoop up center Jesse Sapolu?

   a. 8th

   b. 9th

   c. 10th

   d. 11th

11. How many total games did the 49ers' picks in the 1984 USFL Supplemental Draft end up playing for the franchise?

a. 10
b. 12
c. 14
d. 16

12. The 49ers made three picks in the 3rd round of the 1986 NFL Draft, all of whom started for San Francisco in Super Bowl XXIII.

a. True
b. False

13. The 49ers drafted which current television analyst in the 9th round of the 1991 NFL Draft?

a. Bucky Brooks
b. Michael Strahan
c. Willie McGinest
d. Louis Riddick

14. In 2000, the 49ers drafted which long snapper in the 7th round who went on to tie the franchise record for consecutive games played at 208?

a. Tyrone Hopson
b. Brian Jennings
c. Kory Minor
d. Eric Johnson

15. When was the last time the 49ers did NOT trade one of their draft picks or acquire a different draft pick on draft day?

a. 2003

b. 2004

c. 2006

d. 2007

16. The 49ers drafted Alex Smith with the 1st overall pick in 2005, then followed up by selecting Frank Gore in the 2nd round that same year.

a. True

b. False

17. The 2007 NFL Draft was a successful one for the 49ers, who drafted three players who would end up making a Pro Bowl while in San Francisco. Who was NOT part of that 2007 class?

a. Vernon Davis

b. Patrick Willis

c. Dashon Goldson

d. Joe Staley

18. Which member of the 49ers' starting defensive line from Super Bowl LIV was NOT drafted in the 1st round?

a. Nick Bosa

b. Arik Armstead

c. DeForest Buckner

d. Sheldon Day

19. Before selecting Mike McGlinchey in the 1st round in 2018, who had been the last offensive player San Francisco selected with its first pick of the draft?

a. Carlos Hyde

b. Colin Kaepernick

c. A.J. Jenkins

d. Joe Staley

20. In which round of the 2019 NFL Draft did the 49ers select punter Mitch Wishnowski?

a. 6th

b. 5th

c. 4th

d. 3rd

QUIZ ANSWERS

1. C – Leo Nomellini

2. A – True

3. D – 12

4. B – Harry Babcock

5. B – Earl Morrall

6. D – Lance Alworth

7. B – Cas Banaszek

8. B – Randy Cross and John Ayers

9. C – 3

10. D – 11th

11. A – 10

12. A – True

13. D – Louis Riddick

14. B – Brian Jennings

15. A – 2003

16. B – False

17. A – Vernon Davis

18. D – Sheldon Day

19. C – A.J. Jenkins

20. C – 4th

DID YOU KNOW?

1. With its first pick in the 1983 NFL Draft, the San Francisco 49ers selected a game-changing running back in Roger Craig in the 2nd round. With their final pick, the 49ers drafted an offensive lineman who would go on to be a major cog in three Super Bowl championships. Jesse Sapolu was an 11th round selection out of Hawaii with the 289th overall selection, but ended up starting one game in 1983. He was a backup on the 1984 Super Bowl championship team, but he became a full-time starter in 1987 and helped pave the way for the 49ers' wins in 1988, 1989, and 1994.

2. Another famous 11th round selection for the 49ers was 1977 draftee Brian Billick. The Brigham Young tight end never actually played in the league, but he made a name for himself as a coach in the NFL. He was the head coach of the Baltimore Ravens for nine seasons from 1999-2007, coaching the Ravens to their first Super Bowl title in his second season in the league. Billick had an 85-67 record with Baltimore, including four playoff appearances, and became a television analyst after he was fired from the Ravens.

3. San Francisco has drafted 1st overall three times in franchise history, and each selection has been better than the last one. Harry Babcock played just 30 games in the NFL after being drafted with the top pick in 1955, catching 16 passes for 181

117

yards all with San Francisco. Dave Parks was the 49ers' leading receiver in 1965 after being drafted 1st overall in 1964 and played with the team for four seasons before signing with the New Orleans Saints where he played for five years before finishing his career with Houston. In 2005, the 49ers drafted Alex Smith with that 1st pick, and though he never was elite, he has been a very good quarterback in the league since he was drafted. He was traded to Kansas City in 2013, then traded to Washington in 2018 before suffering a nasty leg injury in a game.

4. Few teams have as much success with their 1st round picks in three consecutive seasons as the 49ers did in their first three drafts as an NFL franchise. San Francisco's first pick in 1950 was Leo Nomellini, the following year it was Y.A. Tittle, and in 1952, it was Hugh McElhenny. That's three Hall-of-Fame selections for the franchise. He wasn't a 1st round pick in 1953, but the 49ers drafted Bob St. Clair in the 3rd round that year, to make it four straight seasons of drafting a Hall-of-Famer. Then, from 1956-58, the 49ers drafted three players who are borderline Hall-of-Famers in the 1st round with Earl Morrall (1956), John Brodie (1957), and Charlie Krueger (1958).

5. San Francisco had a habit of trading its 1st round pick in the mid to late 1970s. The 49ers didn't have a selection in the 1st round in the 1976, 1977, or 1979 Drafts. They were able to draft Randy Cross with their first pick of the 1976 NFL Draft, then later drafted John Ayers in the 8th round that year. But the team struck out in 1977 with none of

their draft picks playing more than 29 games in the NFL. In 1978, San Francisco drafted longtime linebacker Dan Bunz with the second of two 1st round picks, but Ken McAfee, the other pick that year, played just two seasons with the team. Of course, the 49ers were able to get a steal in Joe Montana in the 3rd round of the 1979 Draft to make up for not having a 1st round selection that year.

6. The 49ers didn't have a selection until the 39th overall pick in 1986, but they made the picks they did have count in a big way. Larry Roberts had a serviceable career as San Francisco's 2nd round pick, but it was the next four selections who made the bigger impact on the team. Tom Rathman went off the board to San Francisco 56th overall, and eight picks later, Tim McKyer was selected by the 49ers. John Taylor was the 49ers third 3rd round pick of the draft, setting the table for Charles Haley and Steve Wallace to be drafted in the 4th round by the franchise. Those five players all were primary starters in the NFL for at least seven seasons, and three of them earned Pro Bowl nods in their careers.

7. San Francisco has uncovered several quarterback gems in the later rounds who have gone on to have long careers in the NFL. In 1993, the 49ers drafted Elvis Grbac in the 8th round, and the Michigan product served as Steve Young's backup for three seasons, winning six of his nine starts in that span. He was signed with Kansas City in 1997 and became a regular starter for the Chiefs for four years and with the Ravens for one before retiring. San Francisco also

found value in the 7th round of the 2000 NFL Draft with Louisiana Tech quarterback Tim Rattay. Although he was only 4-12 as a starter with the team, Rattay completed nearly 61% of his passes and threw for almost 4,000 yards in 32 appearances over six years with the team.

8. The 49ers have had a habit of drafting well in the later rounds, but perhaps never fully reaping the benefits of those selections. San Francisco drafted Delanie Walker in the 6th round of the 2006 NFL Draft, but the tight end blossomed when he signed with the Tennessee Titans. In seven years with the Titans, Walker has produced three times as many receiving yards and caught three times as many passes as he did in seven years with the 49ers. It was a similar effect with guard Mike Person, who the 49ers drafted in the 7th round in 2011, then cut right before the season started. He bounced around to five different teams before solidifying himself as a starter, then returning to San Francisco for the final two years of his career.

9. The draft isn't the only place San Francisco has found rookie gems. Free safety Zack Bronson was one of the first undrafted free agents to make an impact on the field for the 49ers. The McNeese State graduate played seven years for the 49ers and had 19 interceptions, seven of which came in 2000. Quarterback Jeff Garcia might be the most famous undrafted free agent the 49ers have signed, with 71 starts and 74 appearances in his five years with the franchise. Other notable undrafted rookie free agents for San Francisco include linebacker Brandon Moore (2002),

cornerback Tramaine Brock (2010), tight end Garrett Celek (2012), and running back Jeff Wilson Jr. (2018).

10. The 49ers acquired a second 1st round pick in the 2020 NFL Draft in the DeForest Buckner trade, but they then traded down one slot with Tampa Bay and drafted South Carolina defensive tackle Javon Kinlaw. San Francisco traded its own 1st round pick to move up to 25th and select Arizona State wide receiver Brandon Aiyuk. The 49ers didn't pick again until the 5th round, selecting West Virginia offensive lineman Colton McKivitz, then drafted Georgia tight end Charlie Woerner in the 6th round. San Francisco finished out the 2020 Draft by picking Tennessee wide receiver Jauan Jennings in the 7th round.

CHAPTER 12:

LET'S MAKE A DEAL

QUIZ TIME!

1. Which running back did San Francisco send Pittsburgh in exchange for Hall-of-Famer John Henry Johnson?

   a. Sam Cathcart

   b. J.R. Boone

   c. John Williams

   d. Ed Pullerton

2. Who did the 49ers acquire when they shipped off Y.A. Tittle to the New York Giants in 1961?

   a. John Wittenborn

   b. Frank Youso

   c. Lou Cordileone

   d. Dick Nolan

3. Which Heisman Trophy winner did San Francisco trade for in 1965 from the St. Louis Cardinals?

   a. Pete Dawkins

   b. Paul Hornung

c. Billy Cannon

d. John David Crow

4. In which round was the draft pick the 49ers had to surrender to get Bob Hayes from the Cowboys in 1975?

   a. 3rd

   b. 4th

   c. 5th

   d. 6th

5. How many draft picks did the 49ers give up in the trade with New England for Jim Plunkett?

   a. 3

   b. 4

   c. 5

   d. 6

6. Which player cost the 49ers a 1st round pick, two 2nd picks, a 3rd round selection, and a 4th round pick in a 1978 trade?

   a. Steve DeBerg

   b. Delvin Williams

   c. Simpson

   d. Freddie Solomon

7. To which team did the 49ers trade their original 3rd round pick to acquire the 82nd overall pick in the 1979 NFL Draft to select Joe Montana?

   a. Dallas Cowboys

   b. Miami Dolphins

   c. Atlanta Falcons

   d. Seattle Seahawks

8. The 1981 trade that brought Fred Dean to San Francisco included a clause that allowed San Diego to flip 1ˢᵗ round picks in the 1983 NFL Draft.

   a. True
   b. False

9. Which offensive tackle did the 49ers acquire from the Raiders in exchange for sending back the 5ᵗʰ round pick San Francisco earned when the Raiders signed Cedrick Hardman in 1980?

   a. Lindsey Mason
   b. Ron Singleton
   c. John Choma
   d. Allan Kennedy

10. Which team originally owned the rights to the draft pick San Francisco used to draft Jerry Rice?

    a. Buffalo Bills
    b. Los Angeles Rams
    c. New England Patriots
    d. Kansas City Chiefs

11. Which draft pick did the 49ers NOT trade to move up to select Jerry Rice in 1985?

    a. 1985 1ˢᵗ round pick
    b. 1986 1ˢᵗ round pick
    c. 1985 2ⁿᵈ round pick
    d. 1985 3ʳᵈ round pick

12. Which two draft picks did the 49ers trade to Tampa Bay in 1987 in exchange for Steve Young?

    a. 1st and 2nd rounds
    b. 2nd and 3rd rounds
    c. 2nd and 4th rounds
    d. 1st and 3rd rounds

13. The 49ers did NOT receive a 1st round draft pick in the trade that sent Charles Haley to Dallas.

    a. True
    b. False

14. Who was the other player San Francisco included in the 1993 trade that sent Joe Montana to Kansas City?

    a. Dana Hall
    b. David Whitmore
    c. Antonio Goss
    d. Bill Romanowski

15. What was the price Miami paid to help San Francisco offload Jim Druckenmiller in 1999?

    a. Two 5th round picks
    b. Two 6th round picks
    c. A 6th and a 7th round pick
    d. Two 7th round picks

16. Which team agreed to send San Francisco a 2004 2nd round draft pick in exchange for Terrell Owens?

    a. Miami Dolphins
    b. Baltimore Ravens

c. Philadelphia Eagles

d. Detroit Lions

17. Which quarterback was sent to the Cleveland Browns as part of the package that brought Trent Dilfer to San Francisco?

a. Cody Pickett

b. Jeff Garcia

c. Ken Dorsey

d. Tim Rattay

18. Which player did San Francisco NOT acquire in exchange for a single draft pick?

a. Dee Ford

b. Anquan Boldin

c. Isaac Bruce

d. Stevie Johnson

19. The Patriots ended up drafting 43rd overall, the 2nd round draft pick the 49ers sent to New England in the Jimmy Garoppolo trade.

a. True

b. False

20. The 49ers moved up in the draft several times over the last decade to grab a player they wanted. For whom did San Francisco NOT move up to draft?

a. DeForest Buckner

b. Colin Kaepernick

c. C.J. Beathard

d. Eric Reid

QUIZ ANSWERS

1. D – Ed Pullerton

2. C – Lou Cordileone

3. D – John David Crow

4. A – 3rd

5. B – 4

6. C – O.J. Simpson

7. D – Seattle Seahawks

8. A – True

9. A – Lindsey Mason

10. C – New England Patriots

11. B – 1986 1st round pick

12. C – 2nd and 4th rounds

13. A – True

14. B – David Whitmore

15. D – Two 7th round picks

16. B – Baltimore Ravens

17. C – Ken Dorsey

18. C – Isaac Bruce

19. B – False

20. A – DeForest Buckner

DID YOU KNOW?

1. The Patriots have supplied the 49ers with several draft picks that turned into key players for San Francisco. In addition to Jerry Rice, the 49ers also acquired a selection from New England to draft Bubba Paris in 1982, Tim Rattay in 2000, and Joe Staley in 2007. The Staley trade involved the 49ers giving New England the 110th pick in the 2007 Draft and their 1st round pick in 2008 in order to get back into the 1st round to draft Staley.

2. The first trades San Francisco made as an NFL franchise came in its inaugural season of 1950. The 49ers sent running back Glenn Davis to the Los Angeles Rams for running back Emil Sitko. In one season with the team, Sitko ran 23 times for 105 yards and a touchdown and caught three passes for 43 yards and two scores. That same year, the 49ers sent a 4th round draft pick to Cleveland for Gordy Soltau, who led the 49ers in scoring every season from 1950 to 1958.

3. The Y.A. Tittle trade in 1961 created a lot of consternation for both players involved in the deal. Tittle was disgusted to be traded for a rookie offensive guard, while Lou Cordileone was upset about being traded for a washed-up quarterback. Neither had any desire to leave their respective cities, but both set off for a new adventure. Tittle solidified his Hall-of-Fame credentials in New York,

while Cordileone spent just one season in San Francisco before bouncing around the NFL.

4. Bob Jury is the safety whose name is lost to history as being part of the deal that brought Joe Montana to San Francisco. The 49ers traded their 3rd round pick to Seattle in 1979 for Jury and Dallas's 1979 3rd round draft pick, which the Seahawks owned. In serendipitous fashion, Seattle opened the 3rd round by selecting linebacker Michael Jackson out of Washington with the 49ers' 3rd round pick, and San Francisco closed the round by drafting Joe Montana.

5. Not that there was any doubt that the 49ers won the Jerry Rice trade with New England, but the Patriots did add an All-Pro player with the draft picks in the deal. The Patriots drafted Trevor Matich—most known now as an ESPN college football analyst—with the 1st round pick from San Francisco and picked Ben Thomas with the 2nd round pick. Those two combined to give the Patriots 45 total games in their careers. However, with the 3rd round selection, New England drafted Audray McMillian, who was First Team All-Pro in 1992, but McMillian never played a down for New England.

6. San Francisco took a twisted road before finally utilizing the 1st round pick the Chiefs sent in the Joe Montana trade. The original selection was 18th overall in the 1st round, but the 49ers flipped that to Phoenix for the 20th pick and the 116th selection in 1993. New Orleans then sent San Francisco the 26th pick and a 3rd round pick (81st overall) in

exchange for that 20th pick. The 49ers selected Dana Stubblefield 26th, traded the 81st pick for a 2nd round selection that they flipped into a 1994 1st round pick that was used in the package to move up and draft Bryant Young in 1994, and San Francisco also drafted Artie Smith 116th in 1993.

7. The 49ers are an active team when it comes to making trades in the 1st round. Since 1993, the 49ers have used their own 1st round pick 15 times in those 28 years, but in four of those years, they also traded for a second 1st round selection. Only once in those 13 years that San Francisco didn't use its own pick did the 49ers not draft in the 1st round. That was in 1996 when the 49ers traded the pick the previous year to move up and select J.J. Stokes in the 1st round.

8. The Terrell Owens deal in 2004 was an odd one for the 49ers. On March 4, 2004, they agreed to send Owens to the Ravens for the 51st pick in the 2004 NFL Draft. However, Owens filed a grievance with the NFL Players Association that would have made him a free agent instead of going to Baltimore. In scramble mode, the 49ers and Ravens added the Eagles into the trade on March 16, and the final deal sent Owens to Philadelphia, the 51st pick back to Baltimore, and defensive lineman Brandon Whiting to San Francisco.

9. San Francisco actually traded both draft picks it received in the Alex Smith deal with Washington. It traded the 2013 2nd round pick to Tennessee, which allowed them to draft

Tank Carradine and Chris Borland. The following year, they traded the other 2ⁿᵈ round pick to Denver, then packaged two of the picks they received in that trade to send to Miami for the 57ᵗʰ pick. The 49ers drafted Carols Hyde with that selection, rounding out the Alex Smith trade tree.

10. The 49ers wasted no time in replacing Joe Staley by acquiring Trent Williams in a trade with Washington. San Francisco sent a 5ᵗʰ round selection in the 2020 NFL Draft and a 3ʳᵈ round pick in the 2021 Draft to Washington in exchange for their franchise left tackle. Williams started 119 of 120 games over nine seasons in Washington, but requested a trade from the team over concerns about the medical attention he received that ended up with him requiring surgery this offseason.

CHAPTER 13:

WRITING THE RECORD BOOK

QUIZ TIME!

1. How many receiving yards is Jerry Rice's record-setting postseason total?

   a. 2,245
   b. 2,278
   c. 2,341
   d. 2,442

2. Jerry Rice also easily holds the record for most career touchdowns in the regular season, with 208. How many of those were not receiving touchdowns?

   a. 8
   b. 9
   c. 10
   d. 11

3. Jerry Rice had a reception in an NFL-record 274 consecutive games.

a. True

b. False

4. There have been 15 players to catch three touchdowns in a playoff game, but Jerry Rice is the only one to do it multiple times. How many times has Jerry Rice tied the league record for single-game touchdown receptions in the postseason?

a. 2

b. 3

c. 4

d. 5

5. How many yards did Jerry Rice gain against the Rams in 1985 to set the single-game mark for most receiving yards in a game by a rookie?

a. 241

b. 226

c. 209

d. 193

6. One of the few 49ers receiving records Jerry Rice doesn't hold, Gene Washington holds the record for highest average reception. How many yards did Washington average for each of his 371 catches?

a. 15.8

b. 16.3

c. 17.2

d. 18.0

7. How long is the 49ers' NFL-record road winning streak?

    a. 16
    b. 17
    c. 18
    d. 19

8. Which quarterback holds the record for most pass attempts in a season?

    a. Steve DeBerg
    b. Steve Young
    c. Joe Montana
    d. Jeff Garcia

9. Who holds the San Francisco record for most career interceptions?

    a. Joe Montana
    b. Steve Young
    c. Y.A. Tittle
    d. John Brodie

10. The 49ers hold the record for largest regular-season comeback.

    a. True
    b. False

11. Who holds the 49ers' record for most rushing touchdowns in a game?

    a. Frank Gore
    b. Colin Kaepernick

c. Joe Perry

d. Billy Kilmer

12. What is the 49ers' record for most touches in a game?

    a. 30

    b. 33

    c. 36

    d. 39

13. The 49ers hold the record for most consecutive games scoring, how long is that record?

    a. 391

    b. 407

    c. 420

    d. 436

14. San Francisco played in the first game that featured zero punts between the two teams.

    a. True

    b. False

15. How many consecutive seasons did the San Francisco 49ers lead the league in scoring to set the longest streak in NFL history?

    a. 3

    b. 4

    c. 5

    d. 6

16. David Akers set the record for most field goals in a season while with the 49ers in 2011. How many did Akers make that season?

   a. 40
   b. 42
   c. 44
   d. 46

17. Who holds the 49ers' record for most career field goal attempts?

   a. Tommy Davis
   b. Ray Wersching
   c. Mike Cofer
   d. Phil Dawson

18. The 49ers hold the record for most consecutive games scoring a field goal.

   a. True
   b. False

19. How many carries did Raheem Mostert need to break the 49ers' postseason single-game rushing mark?

   a. 25
   b. 27
   c. 29
   d. 31

20. Who holds the 49ers' rookie record for passing yards in a season?

a. C.J. Beathard
b. Nick Mullens
c. Alex Smith
d. Steve Young

QUIZ ANSWERS

1. A – 2,245

2. D – 11

3. A – True

4. B – 3

5. A – 241

6. D – 18.0

7. C – 18

8. A – Steve DeBerg

9. D – John Brodie

10. A – True

11. D – Billy Kilmer

12. D – 39

13. C – 420

14. A – True

15. B – 4

16. C – 44

17. A – Tommy Davis

18. B – False

19. C – 29

20. A – C.J. Beathard

DID YOU KNOW?

1. Freddie Solomon's 57-yard punt return for a touchdown was the lone highlight of the first 30 minutes for San Francisco on December 7, 1980. The 0-13 New Orleans Saints came into Candlestick Park and took it to the 49ers, scoring five first-half touchdowns to lead 35-7 at halftime. Perhaps buoyed by an irate Bill Walsh, the 49ers scored two touchdowns in the third quarter and two more in the fourth to force overtime. Joe Montana ran for the first score in the third quarter, then connected on a 71-yard pass to Dwight Clark. He opened the fourth with a 14-yard pass to Solomon, then Lenvil Elliott had a seven-yard run to tie the game. Ray Wersching kicked a 36-yard field goal in overtime to complete the largest regular-season comeback in NFL history.

2. Earlier in that 1980 season, the 49ers suffered the worst loss in franchise history in a 59-14 shellacking at the hands of the Dallas Cowboys. Steve DeBerg completed just 12 of his 35 pass attempts, tossed five interceptions (which isn't the record), and San Francisco lost five fumbles and had just 225 yards of offense. That total was less than 100 yards fewer than what San Francisco gained in its largest victory in franchise history, a 49-0 shutout of the Detroit Lions in 1961. The 49ers ran for six touchdowns that day with two from Billy Kilmer, two from J.D. Smith, and one each from Bob Cooper and Bill Waters. Abe Woodson also returned

the second-half kickoff 98 yards for a touchdown as the 49ers forced six turnovers in the win.

3. From 1977 until 2004—a streak of 420 games that included 26 complete seasons—the 49ers scored at least a point in every game they played. It's a streak that's nearly two full seasons better than second place and one that won't be touched in the near future. It all started after the 49ers lost 7-0 at home to the Atlanta Falcons on October 9, 1977, the second time in the first four games of the 1977 season that San Francisco was shut out. It ended in Seattle on September 26, 2004, when the Seahawks delivered a 34-0 knockout blow. Both games were the fourth game of the season for the 49ers and both sent San Francisco to 0-4 on the season.

4. The second game of the 1992 season sent the two-time reigning AFC champion Buffalo Bills to San Francisco for a potential Super Bowl preview against the 49ers. The Bills escaped on that September 13 day with a 34-31 win in the first game in NFL history without a single punt. The teams combined for more than 1,000 yards of offense, both had three turnovers in the game, and both teams converted on their only fourth-down attempts of the contest. Mike Cofer missed two field goals for the only time a drive didn't end in points, the end of a half or a turnover.

5. David Akers's 2011 season was literally one for the record books, both the 49ers' and the NFL's. In addition to setting the mark for most field goals attempted in a season (52)

and most field goals made in a season (44), Akers's 166 points also set the NFL mark for most points in a season without a touchdown, which is also the 49ers' overall record. Phil Dawson holds the San Francisco record with 14 field goals of 50 yards or more, and Joe Nedney is the most accurate kicker in team history at 86.6% for his 49ers career. Robbie Gould, Jeff Wilkins, and Ray Wersching all share the record by kicking six field goals in a game, which is also the record for most attempts in a game.

6. Steve DeBerg doesn't hold the 49ers' record for most interceptions in a game, but he does hold the record for most interceptions thrown to the 49ers in a game. While he was with the Tampa Bay Buccaneers in 1986, he tossed seven interceptions in a season-opening 31-7 loss to the 49ers in Tampa. Kevin Greene set the record for most sacks against the 49ers with 4.5 in a 1988 game while he was playing for the Rams. Greene would join the 49ers nine years later and register 10.5 sacks in his one season in San Francisco.

7. Gale Sayers holds the record for most touchdowns against the 49ers after scoring six times in a 61-20 Chicago Bears victory in 1965. Sayers ran the ball nine times for 113 yards and four scores, caught a 80-yard touchdown to open the scoring, then returned a punt 85 yards for a touchdown in the fourth quarter. Kurt Warner's 484 passing yards in a 2007 game with the Arizona Cardinals is the record for passing yards against the 49ers. Eight years earlier, Warner threw for five touchdowns as a member of the St.

Louis Rams to tie that 49ers opponent's record with Dan Fouts, Vince Ferragamo, and Donovan McNabb. Isaac Bruce caught four of those touchdowns from Warner in 1999 to tie the mark he shares with Harlon Hill and Ahmad Rashad.

8. Ricky Watters essentially broke the New York Giants in the NFC Divisional round after the 1993 season with 24 carries for 118 yards and a team-record five touchdowns. None of the touchdowns were longer than six yards, but Watters grinded out those yards as the 49ers shut down the Giants 44-3. In fact, Watters's longest run that day was just 20 yards, but it was enough to carry San Francisco into the NFC Championship game.

9. It's rarely a good thing when your quarterback attempts as many passes as you have rushing yards, but it worked out for the 49ers on October 10, 2004. Tim Rattay was forced to throw the ball 57 times against the Arizona Cardinals that day and completed a team-record 38 of them as the 49ers rallied for a 31-28 overtime victory. San Francisco fell behind by 16 points with 8:19 left in the game, but Rattay completed 13 of 19 passes on the final two drives to lead the 49ers to touchdowns. He ran for the first two-point conversion, then threw to Brandon Lloyd for the second. In overtime, he missed on his first three passes, but completed a 23-yard throw to Eric Johnson and a 9-yard toss to Kevan Barlow to set up San Francisco for the winning field goal.

10. Frank Gore might not have the Super Bowl rings, but he is undisputedly the best running back the 49ers have ever had in their backfield. He holds the record for most career rushing yards (11,073) and the most rushing yards in a single season when he ran for 1,695 yards in 2006. He ran for 1,000 yards in eight of his 10 seasons with the team and had 39 100-yard games in 148 appearances—both are records for the franchise. He ran the ball a team-record 2,442 times for San Francisco and ran for a 49ers-record 64 touchdowns. He has two of the 49ers' three 200-yard rushing days in the regular season and holds the team record with five consecutive 100-yard rushing games in 2011.

CONCLUSION

We hope you enjoyed yourself while parsing through the hundreds of facts in this book. Whether you just learned that San Francisco had to make a trade with New England to draft Jerry Rice or thought that question was too easy, hopefully you still had fun quizzing each other throughout the preceding 13 chapters.

Even before they were successful on the field, the 49ers had a rich history in their first two decades with the Million Dollar Backfield and drafting three straight Hall-of-Famers in the first round. The 1970s were a bit of a lull for the team, but since Bill Walsh's arrival in 1979, the San Francisco 49ers have been one of the most relevant teams in the NFL.

They were the first team to win five Super Bowls, doing so in a 15-year span from 1981-95, and have appeared in seven of the 54 Super Bowls played. Some of the best players to ever play in the NFL passed through San Francisco at some point, and some like Joe Montana and Jerry Rice made their names in the Bay Area.

The 49ers' legacy is certainly strong as they embark on the 2020 season and beyond. San Francisco appeared in Super

Bowl XLV, and even held a lead in the fourth quarter. Jimmy Garoppolo is poised to potentially become the next great San Francisco quarterback, and the 49ers' defense is as ferocious as its ever been. One could make a strong argument it's a great time to be a San Francisco 49ers fan.

Manufactured by Amazon.ca
Bolton, ON